COURTING
Trouble

THREE INVITATIONS FROM DEATH

M. A. LEE

Courting Trouble

Three Invitations to Death

Spanish Moss
Texas Sun
Gulf Storm

By

M.A. Lee

WRITERS INK BOOKS

Spanish Moss
Copyright © 2025 Emily Dunn & Writers Ink Books
Texas Sun / Gulf Storm
Copyright © 2025 Emily Dunn & Writers Ink Books

First publishing rights for **Courting Trouble** / 2025
All rights are reserved.

DISCLAIMER
This is a work of fiction. The names, characters, places, and incidents are
products of the writer's imagination or have been used fictitiously and are not to
be construed as real. Any resemblance to persons, living or dead, to actual events
and/or locale or organizations is entirely coincidental. The author does not have
any control over and does not assume any responsibility for third-party websites
or their content. No Artificial Intelligence was used at any time during the
creation or crafting of this work.

First Published in the United States of America
www.writersinkbooks.com

Contents

.~.~.~.~.~.

COURTING TROUBLE BOOK 1

M. A. LEE

Spanish Moss

1 ~ The Death

In all her years as Hyatt Ingram's private secretary, Nedda Courtland had disagreed with several of his decisions but never more so than when he was dying.

She'd returned from delivering his grandson Colfax to the Sacred Heart Academy and found him confined to his deathbed. He ignored his doctor's advice to stay calm and quiet. He commanded his third wife to leave his bedchamber. He demanded that Louisiana Oil Company not delay the upcoming vote on investments from his company Ingram & Son.

His son Sheridan, though, was half-a-continent away, in California.

Had he contacted his son about his failing health? No. Had he notified his grandson Colfax or his secretary Nedda? No. He expected everything to follow the schedule.

Nedda did her job by restoring order to the swirling chaos. The maid stopped flapping about and hied to the kitchens to have a medicinal *tisane* prepared. The manservant came out of his corner and helped adjust the pillows and straighten the bedcovers, trying to make Mr. Ingram comfortable. The doctor drew Nedda into the suite's central reception to convey his diagnosis. Then he retreated with a murmured "Matter of hours, Miss Courtland, not days."

In all his years, no matter how dire the situation, Mr. Ingram had never fretted. Perching on the side of his expansive bed, Nedda covered his writhing hands with her own. His skin felt dry, papery. His eyes were bleary and reddened. His extreme pallor and shortened breaths worried her more than the doctor's diagnosis.

He looked up at her and swallowed, an effort.

"I will get you some water."

"No." His fingers tightened on hers. "Colfax?"

"Settled at the Academy."

"Problems?"

"None, sir."

"You'll need to wire Sheridan."

A wire rather than a telephone call. The old man knew his son would be difficult to contact. "I will have them bring a telephone into the suite. When he rings, you can speak with him."

He huffed, lost his breath, then grabbed at it with rapid inhalations. When his breathing was steady, he asked, "You have his proxy?"

Mr. Ingram knew that she did. They had talked about the proxy numerous times on the train from San Francisco. He had discussed how she would need to vote for Sheridan in the investment meeting with LOC. She also had Sheridan's power of attorney, for she had needed both documents to enroll Colfax in the Sacred Heart Academy. Nedda peered into her employer's eyes and saw a vagrant confusion that she'd missed earlier.

And that's when she knew the doctor's diagnosis was correct.

"Mr. Ingram, what happened? You were not ailing when I left with Colfax, five days ago."

He licked his dry lips. His eyes slewed sideways, to the manservant standing quietly.

"Bring Mr. Ingram a brandy," she ordered with brisk efficiency.

"Miss Courtland, you're in America now," the manservant protested. Hired on their arrival in New Orleans, he thought he needed to explain the laws of the United States to these British visitors. "We're under Prohibition here. Where in this town am I to find brandy?"

"I am certain you can locate a place. The concierge should know a source."

"The doctor said——."

"Given the diagnosis, I hardly think that a brandy will injure Mr. Ingram's health." She waited until the chamber door shut before checking his pulse. His heart fluttered rapidly, faintly. "Tell me."

"Poison."

The word shocked her, but she didn't doubt it. In their travels for Ingram & Son Investments, they'd seen many odd and unexplainable things, especially in Arabia and the Orient. Mr. Ingram believed someone had poisoned him, and she didn't question that belief. His body might fail him, but his mind was still sharp, still penetrating, still seeing traps and snares that other businessmen missed.

Hyatt Ingram had used those wits to amass a substantial fortune long before Nedda encountered him, and he had tripled it since the Great War ended, investing in the worldwide petroleum industry.

She did have one question. "Has the doctor——?"

"Didn't believe me. Says my heart was weak. He listens to Giselle." He had to pause between each statement and gather strength.

Giselle, his third wife—the new bride. A mistake in Arizona that Mr. Ingram had enjoyed making. He'd shared with Nedda that the marriage wouldn't last more than three years. She hadn't thought it would last a year. Giselle hooked him in San Francisco and spent her last dime to follow them to Phoenix where they married. He wanted to be her savior, yet he knew she loved his wallet, not him.

Nedda shook herself mentally. "Do you think she—?"

"Think it was that cicisbeo Clement LaFoy or the accountant or that lawyer LaFoy brought in or that wildcatter."

His eyes drifted closed, giving her a chance to mull over his claim.

That tight little circle had formed since their arrival in New Orleans. The suave LaFoy represented Louisiana Oil, where Jamison Parker was chief accountant, financial advisor, and a guarantor with the local banks. Hank McElroy represented the other petroleum company, the wildcatter firm Texas Petroleum and Refining. The lawyer Henderson Beaumont III was intended to be a neutral party, overseeing the negotiations that would be presented at the LOC meeting where the owners and chief officers would vote on investments from Ingram & Son and from the Texas firm. Ingram had squeaked into LOC two years ago with a financial investment that stabilized the company after a boom-and-bust cycle, and now he had privileges to vote for his increased ownership of the company.

Sly man.

Not sly enough to anticipate a threat. Not savvy enough to avoid poison.

She looked through the open balcony doors. The suite on the top floor gave a view beyond the surrounding buildings. On a far street, the canopy of an old live oak peered above the roofs. Even at this distance, she could see the clusters of Spanish moss draping the boughs. A breeze drifted in, warm in these days of Spring although the natives claimed it was cold.

Nedda envisioned that aged live oak, its massive trunks braced on the ground, bent at crooked angles. The crimped moss looked like the hoary beards of old men.

And the ground underneath would be littered with blackened acorns.

LaFoy and Beaumont. Parker and McElroy. Were they the limbs of a conspiracy to drive Ingram & Son Investments out of LOC?

Or did one of the four men act alone?

Or was it Giselle and LaFoy?

Or someone she didn't know to suspect?

They all received a black mark on the mental tally Nedda was keeping.

"Had a solicitor brought in."

She quickly turned back to Mr. Ingram. His eyes still looked bleary, but his gaze was sharp, watching her, telling her what she needed to know. "A solicitor? Mr. Beaumont?"

"No, not that fool. Alexander Chatto."

"A new will?" she guessed.

His clutch felt slippery, as if his muscles were sliding out of his control. "You have Sheridan's proxy for dealing with Colfax?" he asked again. "You'll have to act for me as well."

"Where is this new will?"

"Chatto has it. He's only to give a copy to you or my son."

"And Giselle?"

The corner of his lip lifted, a simple indication that meant he'd set an unexpected trap. "She'll have her portion, but she won't be getting her fingers into my company."

Voices in the outer reception reached them, a woman and a man then another man.

A knock on the chamber door. Mr. Ingram released her hand and touched a finger to his lip.

She nodded then stood and smoothed down her skirt.

The manservant came in with the brandy.

Mr. Ingram shot a hard glance at Nedda. "I'll rest now. I'm tired."

That dismissed her, but she didn't intend to return to her own room on a lower floor. Five days away meant a backlog of work for her, correspondence and wires and more. Much would become unnecessary were Mr. Ingram to die.

She wanted to think more about this poison. If they knew what kind of poison, the doctor might save Mr. Ingram.

Or not.

She composed her face and went out to Giselle and Clement LaFoy, a convenient paramour since he had tight connections to Louisiana Oil.

One glance revealed the reason Hyatt Ingram had married Giselle Hampton. The platinum blonde was stunning even when her makeup was not immaculate. She wore a shimmering silk day dress in the current flapper style. With her hair coifed in a fluffy bob, her mouth shaped into a Cupid's bow, mascara making her wide blue eyes dramatic, she was a porcelain doll that deserved her place on the shelf where her husband's money would have kept her.

Two porters bowed as they collected tips from her for the dozen packages they had carried into the room. The name of a fashionable boutique was scrolled across several. Nedda said nothing, but Giselle sprang to her own defense. "Just fancy! They have styles direct from Paris."

Clement LaFoy finished lighting a cigarette for Giselle. He placed it in a silvered holder and passed it to the woman. "I doubt Miss Courtland would recognize *avant garde* style, my dear."

Nedda managed to hide a wince, for she loved fashion. Her job enabled occasional indulgences, Chanel or Lanvin or Molyneux, as long as the clothes fit her taste and Mr. Ingram's strict requirements for an unobtrusive secretary.

LaFoy dropped into a club chair and swung one leg over the other. He looked elegant in a silvery suit and mauve tie. He pomaded his black hair and affected a hairline mustache. From the beginning she found him slick as a cat and unconcerned as long as the world didn't touch him. She had never liked cats.

He blew a smoke ring then asked, "How is Colfax? How much did he protest that school?"

Colfax was an English youth stuffed into a Catholic boarding school in an extremely rural parish of Louisiana. He should have been with his peers at Harrow or Eton, but his father had wanted time with the boy after returning from the war. Six years had now passed, and still Colfax traveled with the Ingram men. Yet his father was currently still in San Francisco and his grandfather, hale a week ago, was now failing.

A prominent bishop of San Francisco wrote a letter of introduction for the Anglican youth, but it was the substantial donation that won him admission into the Sacred Heart Academy, for even the half-year mark was well past. Colfax had been on his best behavior when introduced to the headmaster and a couple of the deans. He politely thanked her for her role in winning him entry.

She had misliked his bland expression.

When deeply bored, Colfax was known for pranks. She wasn't certain the academy was prepared for him.

Yet neither Giselle nor LaFoy had ever considered Colfax. The question was meant to fill the air. Nedda gave it the response it deserved rather than the truth. "I think he will find it an interesting interlude."

LaFoy tapped ash from his cigarette onto a crystal tray on a polished ebony side table. "He'll enjoy himself, off his grandfather's leash."

Giselle was opening boxes, flinging the lids to the floor followed by the tissues that had protected the gowns. She lifted out a black silk shimmering with beads then dropped it to pick up a pale pink confection with a dropped waist fitted at the hip and lace overlaying the underskirt. "This one is for dancing tonight in the Blue Room. Have you danced there yet, Miss Courtland? Oh, you wouldn't have, without an escort, would you? It is glorious."

Nedda sidestepped a wafting tissue. "When did Mr. Ingram take a turn for the worse?"

Giselle peered into a rainbow beaded bag and didn't bother to answer. LaFoy blew smoke toward Nedda. "He woke ill the morning after you left with the boy."

If she closed her eyes, she could see the country roads she'd traveled to and from the Academy, with the hard-packed dirt, the oaks leaning over, branches intertwined into an eternal canopy, and ashy green moss swaying in the breeze. "Did you wire Mr. Sheridan Ingram about his father's condition?"

"I knew you would do it upon your return," and Giselle dismissed the question.

Five days. Two days to travel on narrow roads in a rattling touring car that she could walk faster than it drove, a day for all the paperwork to enroll Colfax and see him settled, another two days to return. "Mr. Ingram is gravely ill. The doctor said his condition will only worsen. And you did not think it vital to contact his only son? Mr. Sheridan could have been here by now."

"I didn't have his address" was her excuse.

Nedda narrowed her eyes. The wife obviously didn't want the son here.

Did Giselle know about the lawyer Mr. Ingram had called in?

She could do nothing about the damage to his health that had already occurred. She could only prevent more damage.

Sheridan would need a wire this evening. Only God knew how long it would take to reach him.

Colfax, a youth alone among strangers, would need a warning wire. The wording would have to be delicate. And it might not reach him until morning. The academy had a strict curfew.

Nedda would send the wires before seeking her dinner. Then, although tired from travel, she would return to the suite and tuck into the backlog of work.

And hopefully have more conversation with Mr. Ingram, out of the hearing of his wife and the manservant.

The only problem with Nedda's vow to safeguard Mr. Ingram was that he died in the overnight.

2 ~ The Will

Nedda's second wire to Sheridan Ingram was stark.

Father deceased Stop Instructions Needed Stop

She didn't wire the solicitors that the Ingrams used in London. She wouldn't until the new will was a certainty. Nor did she send a wire to Colfax. A fifteen-year-old boy did not need to learn of his grandfather's death through a telegram. She called the academy, and after a long wrangle with the headmaster, Colfax came on the line.

After her careful announcement, he said nothing for a long minute then, "Was he in pain? At the end?"

Nedda swallowed her first words. "Mr. Ingram was sleeping when he passed away."

"Oh. Then——. That's—that's good." Another long pause then he asked, "Did he know?"

She sidestepped his grandfather's claim of poison. That would be impossible to prove now. All she could do was block whatever plan the murderer had made. "I believe he knew."

"That must have ... frustrated him."

The youth knew his grandfather very well. Business swirled around him, in part because Mr. Ingram would stir it up whenever he became bored. Her only answer could be "Yes. Colfax, do you wish to attend his funeral? We can delay it until you arrive, but your—your stepgrandmother wishes to have the service quickly. On Sunday."

"No. No, I don't want to remember him in a casket or see him lowered into the ground."

They interred the dead aboveground in New Orleans, but Colfax didn't need to have that image for his imagination to work upon, not with this shock of his grandfather's death.

"Do you want me to speak with you after? I will."

"No. Write me a letter after. You write good letters, Miss Courtland. I-I'll miss——." He choked.

She waited, but he didn't finish that sentence. She began tentatively, "You might speak with a priest."

"Not here. Not now. Thank you for ringing me, Miss Courtland."

"Colfax——. I will pray for you."

"I don't need your prayers, Miss Courtland. Maybe pray for my father. Does he know?"

"I wired him. He hasn't responded."

"*She* didn't?"

She could only mean Giselle. "No."

"She wouldn't," and with that, the youth revealed how much he understood about his step-grandmother. "Goodbye, Miss Courtland."

"Goodbye, Colfax. Please have the headmaster come back to the telephone."

Father Ignatius promised to keep a closer watch on Colfax. He waited for the boy to leave his office before he added, "Grief can be a strange thing, Miss Courtland. One handles the occurrence of a death in a stoic manner only for grief to break out in unexpected ways weeks and weeks after. We know the signs to look for. You will also be experiencing grief, Miss Courtland, especially as you had only a few hours to realize Mr. Ingram's condition. We shall add you to our prayers."

"Thank you, Father." She rang off.

Nedda had to dab tears from her eyes before she left the call box, tucked to one side of the hotel's lobby. She checked the time and realized her watch had wound down.

Hank McElroy found her there, standing in the middle of the lobby as guests and porters flowed around her, trying to wind her watch while tears blurred her eyes.

"Miss Courtland, I'm pleased to see you back." Then he saw her brimming eyes and her pallor. "Here now, what's up?"

He was a blur to her, but she recognized that drawl in a gruff voice. "Mr. McElroy. Oh."

He took the watch from her shaky hands. "What's happened? Something dire must have, to disturb that English cool."

Nedda caught back a sob, refusing to give in to emotions before strangers, especially this man, a roughneck oil driller. In all the debates over the negotiations with Louisiana Oil, he had remained unfazed. Even Mr. Ingram had lost his vaunted sangfroid a couple of times, when Clement LaFoy had tried to add restrictions on the investment vote, wanting to separate the owners' voting into two days. Under LaFoy's plan, they would vote on investment from Texas Oil and Refining three days before voting on Ingram & Son Investments.

She knew no other way to tell him than the basic truth. "Mr. Hyatt Ingram died this morning."

"Yep, they told me that. Said Mrs. Ingram won't accept visitors yet."

"She cannot accept visitors. She's gone shopping. She has nothing suitable for a funeral." The widow's actions still appalled her.

He grasped her elbow in his large, capable hand, warm against her chilled skin. "Let's get out of the way. Over here." He steered her out of the walking traffic and toward a seating area at the back of the lobby, overlooking a green space behind the hotel.

Without quite knowing how, Nedda found herself in a deeply cushioned chair, seated in sunshine flooding through the windows, cracked enough to catch a breeze. Birdsong flooded in, loud and melodious.

Mr. McElroy gave a soft command of "stay put" and left. It was easier to obey. She touched her much-abused handkerchief to her eyes, worried about the state of her mascara, then refused to think about it any more.

Spanish moss dangled from the arching branches of a young tree. A gray gnatcatcher clung to the sagey moss as it hunted insects.

Mr. McElroy returned, a porter with a tray of coffee behind him.

Nedda would have preferred tea, but she took the steaming cup then held it close. The brew's aroma shoved a few supports under her odd weakness.

Hank McElroy lowered his long frame into a nearby chair, angled toward her, with his own steaming cup. He sipped then grimaced. "Can never get used to the chicory they use here. When did you get back from dealing with the grandson?"

"Last evening."

"You saw Ingram then, before——."

"Yes." She didn't mention the claim of poison. She sipped the coffee, so hot it nearly burnt her tongue. Ingram's claim could not be proved. The doctor would not support a claim—and may have even supplied whatever poison was used. Digitalis, at a guess, an increase in dosage, for the life-saving heart drug became lethal at the wrong dose.

"Now there's that mind at work."

Startled, she glanced at Mr. McElroy. In all their encounters during the negotiations, she'd served as secretary to Mr. Ingram. She didn't think he'd paid any attention to her at all. His eyes were down, watching the spin of the watch hands as he set it to the time matching his watch. In his sun-tanned hands, her silver watch looked fragile and glistening bright.

"I suppose you informed the boy."

"Yes, and Father Ignatius at the Academy. I sent a wire to his son in California."

"When can we expect him?"

"I would not hazard a guess. He said he would be hunting in the mountains. I do not even know when he will receive my wire."

He handed over her watch. When she fumbled to latch it, he stood and gathered up her wrist and the watch in gentle hands. He bent to the task. She saw the long angle of his nose, crooked near the bridge, and that square jaw and his tousled dark hair. She murmured her thanks as he straightened, task done, and he returned to his seat and his coffee.

"They'll be pushing to get him in the ground, Miss Courtland. Mrs. Ingram will want the will probated."

"That cannot happen until we return to London—oh. He has a new will," she recalled with a sinking heart. She knew the contents of the old will. The majority of the estate and the entail devolved to his son, with a substantial bequest to Colfax. At age 25, the boy would be independent of his father's purse-strings. A widow's portion would go to the second and third wives. Mr. Ingram had written a bequest for her and his primary caregivers of the London house. Had he changed that in his new will? "He hired a lawyer here to write it for him, while I was gone with Colfax. A Mr. Alexander Chatto."

"Alejandro Chatto," he corrected. "I brought the man to Mr. Ingram. That was the day after he first fell ill. Chatto handles legal business for me and the firm here in Louisiana."

She covered her surprise at his help to Mr. Ingram with a sidestep. "I thought your business was based in Texas."

He grinned, light eyes bright. "My business is oil, Miss Courtland, wherever that takes me. Right now, it brings me into Louisiana. Might take me to Alaska. Definitely into some countries well south of here."

"Caddo Lake?" she hazarded. "And other points around the Gulf?"

"Now I knew you were a sharp one." He refreshed his coffee from the pot. With raised eyebrows and a lift of the pitcher, he asked if she wanted more. Nedda shook her head. He took up his cup, fragile china cupped in his entire hand. "You'll need to see Chatto. His office is at Dumaine and Chartres. Why don't I find us a taxi while you freshen up?"

That reminded her of the devastation that tears could wreck on mascara.

. ~ . ~ . ~ .

Alejandro Chatto's office was off Chartres Street on Dumaine. Elegant ironwork on balconies and windows graced the façade of the blue-washed building. The windows stood open to catch the morning breeze. Nearby, the great Mississippi River snaked its way to the Gulf of Mexico.

Mr. McElroy presented her to Mr. Chatto, a classic Creole like Clement LaFoy, only he didn't pomade his dark hair or smoke constantly or concentrate on her assets. His suit was classic dark, with sharp lapels and an understated waistcoat and a diamond-patterned dark tie. The lawyer introduced his secretary Mrs. Copper, grey-haired in a tight bun, wearing a starched blouse in pale blue with a darker blue skirt. Her fingers were poised above the typewriter keys, a position Nedda knew very well, too much to type and little time to accomplish it. Introductions made, Mr. McElroy waited in the anteroom while the lawyer escorted her into his office.

Sunshine warmed the room, touching on dark furniture, a heavy knee-hole desk, barrister bookcases, a side table before the open balcony windows, and two chairs, half-upholstered, angled in front of the desk. Only the floor didn't speak the seriousness of law but was painted in a green-and-white checkerboard, scuffed over the years. The stout door muted the clacking of the typewriter.

Mr. Chatto's desk backed upon the sunniest window, giving him an unfair advantage over visitors, for his face would be in shadow.

She approved.

He wanted her identification. Nedda handed over her much-used passport and the card given her in San Francisco, to allow her to chauffeur Mr. Ingram. Mr. Chatto lifted his eyebrows at the California license then flicked through several stamped pages of her passport.

He placed them on his desk within her reach and leaned back in his chair. "You are much traveled, Miss Courtland."

"I have served as Mr. Ingram's personal secretary for over a decade."

"He trusted you. I am instructed, by him, to show the will to you and no other before I file it in Succession, Probate you will likely call it. I suppose the doctor did not provide a death certificate to you."

"That is to be delivered this afternoon to the hotel. Mrs. Ingram was most insistent."

He studied her. Nedda wasn't certain what he had expected of a secretary to a wealthy financier. By noon, the news of Hyatt Ingram's death would flash around the world. With the will in hand, or a copy of it, she would wire his attorneys in London. They would know to contact the myriad businesses that Mr. Ingram had delved into since the Great War. Any partners, always shaky at change, would want to know how his death would affect their companies. No one but Sheridan would concern themselves with Ingram & Son Investments.

In the past years, his son had become his right-hand. Giselle hadn't met Sheridan, but she was aware of the various roles he performed for his father. Sheridan knew of the new wife, for Nedda had wired him on the evening of the wedding.

Father Re-married Stop Giselle Hampton Starlet
Stop Questions? Stop

Sheridan responded.

Congratulations to my Father Stop

She supposed a third wife didn't really surprise him.

But she wished he were here, not in California. He had a better right to ask questions of how a man as healthy as Hyatt Ingram was on Sunday could be so debilitated in two days then dead within a week.

"You are not what I expected, Miss Courtland," the lawyer said, jerking her from her memories.

Nedda picked up her identification and returned the documents to her purse. "How is that, Mr. Chatto?"

"Frankly, I expected an older woman. Ingram gave me to understand that you controlled the world at your fingertips."

She raised her eyebrows. "Hardly that, sir. Modern conveniences have merely brought the world closer."

"Efficient, effective, exceptional. His three words, mind you, when I asked him if you would be a capable executrix."

The flattery disconcerted her. She could only respond with "Mr. Ingram surrounds himself with reliable people. Surrounded," she amended. "The will?"

"I will provide you an unsigned copy of the will, for your benefit. My secretary is typing a copy for Mr. Sheridan Ingram to receive—if you have his address."

"Mr. Ingram the younger was last at the Fairmount Hotel in San Francisco. A letter directed to him there would reach him, as he intended it to be his base while he ventured around northern California, but I do hope that his father's death means that he has begun his journey here. Perhaps you should retain that copy for him."

Mr. Chatto murmured assent before he drew out a jangling set of keys. He selected a silvery one and unlocked the top left drawer of his desk. The will was folded into a blue envelope. He also handed over a sealed letter. "Mr. Hyatt Ingram dictated this to me after we finished signing the will."

Her name looped across the letter's envelope in a fair copperplate hand. She opened the letter first. A more spidery scrawl fitted two pages. That also wasn't Mr. Ingram's precise, tight handwriting, but that was certainly his signature at the end, with the date three days before and a time of late afternoon. Below that was a statement and signature, Chatto's, stating that Hyatt Ingram had dictated the letter to him.

And beneath was a witness signature. Hank McElroy.

She raised her eyebrows in a mute question, but the lawyer consulted documents on his desk, giving her a modicum of privacy.

Nedda scanned the letter, saving a closer perusal for when she was entirely alone.

Mr. Ingram's decisive mind came through the written words. She was to be executrix for him; his son's arrival would not change that. He could not recall all of his bequests from his previous will, but he had provided a lump sum for her to disperse based on those previous instructions. Nedda had a brief memory of those bequests—to his London valet and the housekeeper and the butler, pretty stipends that would pension them nicely.

He trusted that she would advise his son of all business dealings in Texas and Louisiana when Sheridan finally arrived from California. Then he had slyly dictated, "You will take action as you have been, Miss Courtland; we place our trust in you."

He didn't mention the proxy. Shrewd as he was, he knew some of his current fellows in this petroleum project might want to play hopscotch with the substantial funds he'd already turned over to Louisiana Oil. Mr. Ingram's reason for keeping the proxy quiet seemed wise—and with the vote coming next week, if Sheridan didn't arrive soon, she would have to use it.

Last of all, he said he had a surprise for his current wife.

He must have discovered her infidelity.

The will itself was a dry document, with all of the correct forms. Mr. Ingram had remembered the main bequests: his son to receive the estate and the bulk of his fortune, a trust fund that would pay for Colfax's education and business ventures well into his 40's unless he ran wild with the money. In addition, Sheridan would have the Mayfair place in Grosvenor Square while Colfax received a small *pied à terre* in Chelsea, former residence of Mr. Ingram's late aunt.

And there she was, executrix and with a bequest that widened her eyes, triple what had merely been a lovely independence in the former will. Another lump sum placed in her name had the purpose of payment of bequests to his intended pensioners, as named in the previous will.

Ah, here was the surprise. Mr. Ingram's second wife, Lady Clare Whitgate Ingram, would receive a substantial sum for three years, the amount similar to before. Giselle would not be that fortunate. The new widow would have to receive something, but Mr. Ingram reduced the amount by three-fourths—and added a dry comment that her "present beloved would doubtless provide a long-term support to Giselle Hampton."

Mr. Ingram hadn't mentioned the shares in Ingram Investments that he'd turned over to Lady Clare as part of their divorce settlement. Those shares ensured a princely sum to Lady Clare every year. Giselle would not receive any shares.

Nedda smiled at that. She could hear the echo of Mr. Ingram's voice, that sly tone when he sprang a trap that no one had expected.

The rest of the will had no surprises ... except in the number of witnesses, four. Three didn't surprise her: Florence Copper, Mr. Chatto's secretary; Jamison Parker, the accountant for Louisiana Oil; and Felix Vaccaro, one of the owners of Roosevelt Hotel.

The name that surprised her was Hank McElroy.

His name again as witness to these documents.

When and how had he earned Mr. Ingram's trust?

3 ~ The Way

"You have to eat, and you might as well eat with me." Hank McElroy's rough persuasion had more influence than a smoother demand. "Not here at the hotel, though. Everyone will be watching, thinking you know the dead man."

Nedda winced at that brutal honesty, but he was right, so she agreed.

"A pretty dress."

"I will not. This is not a celebration."

"Something nice," he amended. "It's not a lunch counter I'm taking you to."

"Something nice," she repeated, and he left her in the lobby.

She watched him stride through the glass and brass doors then turned away. Foolish dreams weren't for her. She was a professional woman, well into her late twenties.

The hotel served a heavy lunch in the main dining room, but three weeks ago she had found a smaller dining room which served a light lunch, salad and poached fish with fruit for dessert. She ordered tea then composed a wire to Devensay, Pethbridge, and Frederick, Solicitors, London.

She didn't want to tell the firm too much information. They only needed three facts, of Mr. Ingram's death, of the new will, and of her role as executrix. She didn't expect a reply, for one o'clock here would be six o'clock in London.

The solicitors were careful and conservative in their responses to actions Mr. Ingram proposed. Worse would be a delayed response whenever he'd taken an action they found risky. Devensay, Pethbridge had waited a solid twenty-four hours before responding to news of his marriage to Giselle Hampton. They had offered to write a codicil to his will, but he had refused that, saying that he didn't expect a quick return to London. He claimed that the statement in the will about his wife, unnamed, would serve for both his second and his third wives. When the solicitors protested, he retorted, "My bank account will cover the bequests to both women."

After sending the wire, she retreated to her room, wanting privacy for her closer reading of his letter and the new will. Only then did she release the tears that had wanted to pour out since morning.

A knock caught her when she was mopping up. Drying her eyes with another tissue, she opened the door to a young porter in the hotel livery.

"Telegram for Miss Nedda Courtland. Sign here, please." He flipped open a notebook and handed her a fountain pen. Once she signed and returned his pen, he produced the wire from the back of the notebook, touched his cap, and tripped away.

Nedda stared at the envelope as she closed the door. She fetched a letter opener from the travel case that she'd converted to business use.

Devensay, Pethbridge had spent a pretty penny on this wire.

```
   Received Information in Afternoon Financial News
  Stop Devensay Four in New York City Stop Traveling
    to You on Morrow Stop Arrives in Two Days Stop
   Crescent Train from New York Stop Take No Action
  until Devensay Four Sees New Will Stop Try to Delay
             Vote Stop Sympathy to Widow
```

She giggled at the wire. Never had the firm responded so quickly.

Devensay Four was Peter Devensay, in his late forties and the fourth generation of the founder, a son in the mold of the Devensay line.

She sobered. From what she had gleaned from the doctor's conversation with Giselle this morning, the funeral would be in two days. She didn't think it could be delayed. Mr. Devensay would arrive that evening, missing the funeral.

She found the L & N Timetable, flipped the page for the Crescent Line, and confirmed her memory. He would miss the funeral.

His concern would be the new will, of course.

Did Giselle know about the new will? She didn't know the contents of the old will, only that she would receive a widow's portion while the bulk of the estate would devolve to Ingram's only son. Would she make trouble about Sheridan's inheritance?

If he ever arrived.

Clement LaFoy might instigate such trouble.

The accountant Jamison Parker had witnessed the will. He might not know the particulars of the will. His first loyalty was to Louisiana Oil Company. And LaFoy also worked for LOC.

Like Ingram, LaFoy seemed to be a new investor in LOC. Hank McElroy worked for Texas P & R, which wanted to increase investment in LOC, the same financial arrangement that Mr. Ingram had proposed. McElroy was some sort of executive; she had never been able to pin down his exact role. Did an executive in a wildcatter company mean the same thing as executive in a conservative, established company?

She had her orders, though, direct from Mr. Ingram. Prevent any delay in the vote. Guard Mr. Ingram's finances and his company.

Devensay, Pethbridge wanted her to delay the vote and let Mr. Devensay make decisions about the new will.

She hoped Peter Devensay and Alejandro Chatto found each other *simpatico.*

. ~ . ~ . ~ .

Nedda nearly cried again as she dressed for dinner with Mr. McElroy.

The chandelier earrings nearly broke her. Mr. Ingram had gifted them on the last anniversary of her hiring, a date he'd never forgotten. He rewarded loyalty, and for her tenth year in his employ, he'd given her earrings centered with black onyx and three dangling diamond strands. He had called the earrings a trifle, but the appraised value meant they had to be insured.

They were worthy of her Chanel ribbon dress and her ribbon-strap black heels. Last thing, she added the earrings. As she screwed them on, she had to blink rapidly to stop the tears from ruining her makeup.

Hank McElroy's appreciative look was worth her trouble.

As they crossed the lobby, she spied Giselle Ingram on Clement LaFoy's arm, entering the hotel restaurant. She wore a black frock covered with beading, one of today's purchases, to have clothes appropriate for a widow.

"I thought Broussard's," Mr. McElroy said when the taxi started forward. "They have quiet corner tables although that dress—you deserve center stage."

The flattery seemed wrong with Mr. Ingram's death so fresh. *This very morning*, she realized and caught her breath.

"We'll keep quiet then," he said then began pointing out landmarks of the Vieux Carré.

Broussard's had patrons waiting, but they maneuvered past. True to McElroy's word, the host escorted them to a corner table, away from the kitchen. While she perused the menu, he asked her preferences, narrowing her choices. The waiter appeared, very stiff in his white jacket, and he ordered quickly, sending the man off.

He tugged at his tie, a first sign of discomfort in his black suit. He didn't seem a man for tuxedoes and elegant dinners that lasted all evening.

Nedda tucked her beaded purse on her lap and leaned forward. "Borrowed or rented?"

He gave that endearing lopsided grin. "Bought," he answered, not pretending to misunderstand nor be perturbed by her query. "Three hours of my afternoon gone for the fitting."

"The effort is appreciated but unnecessary." She glanced at the diners around them. "Most of the men are wearing dark suits."

"I had a feeling you would come out in something grand. You deserved an escort to match."

"And how would you guess that?"

His grin broadened. "First time I saw you, you had one of those glossy fashion magazines, flipping through it, while Ingram read through some documents."

She remembered that day, hot for spring, especially as they were seated on a bench outside a shack that served as an on-shore office for the oil rigs at Caddo Lake. Inside had been airless and thick with humidity. Outside was the assault of birds screeching in the moss-covered trees and the steady hum and creaks of the rig motors on the lake. On that day his light blue eyes had pierced her soul. His slow grin and easy replies to Mr. Ingram's snapped comments had impressed her. Mr. Parker had seemed agitated by Mr. Ingram's brusque queries for information. Hank McElroy answered in a soft drawl that lacked intimidation of the wealthy Englishman.

"You were there with that accountant," she recalled. "Jamison Parker."

"Waiting for LaFoy and his lawyer to show," he drawled. That Texas accent, slow but steady, seeped into her like the black gold stolen from the ground.

"Beaumont the Third," she murmured.

"Yep."

"Tell me about them. LaFoy and Beaumont and Parker. And you, Mr. McElroy. I know what Mr. Ingram knew, but I believe I should know more."

"Seeing as how you've got the younger Ingram's voting proxy. That wife of his know that?"

"Not . . . yet."

He gave another grin. "I want to be there for that ruckus." Then he leaned back, a sommelier poured white wine, and a waiter served a potage of creole fish.

Nedda hadn't realized how they had both leaned closer over the table to talk. As soon as the servers left, Hank McElroy leaned forward again, and she found herself matching him.

He gave a succinct precis of each man, sharp as a lawyer or a financier. He stopped to sip his wine, and she prompted, "And you?"

His light blue eyes remained steady on her dark eyes. "Cool English, aren't you? Thinking about Ingram's claim?" Then he launched into his background, how he entered the oil business and how he'd turned wild-catting into steady work that survived the boom-and-bust that bankrupted so many.

"Too much dry talk," he said, drinking the red cabernet that had replaced the white. "Sweet's coming, and it's your turn to talk. How did you get on with Ingram?"

The hour was late when they left Broussard's, but Bourbon Street was in full display, merry-goers singing in the streets, ladies on balconies calling down to men, music pouring out of the bars and speakeasies. Here, Prohibition had never occurred.

Then she saw an odd sign, little but blatant red, posted on a mustard-painted door a few steps down from the restaurant.

She stayed Mr. McElroy's amble with a tug on his arm.

His gaze followed her pointing finger, and he inhaled deeply before shaking his head. "Forgot that was here."

"Did you?"

"Well, now, maybe I remembered earlier, but I forgot later."

She believed that.

"Voodoo," he warned.

"Take me."

He studied her then flicked her earrings. "These come off."

She removed them and tucked them deep into her purse. He was shifting his hand in his trouser pocket, moving his wallet.

"Stay close."

She gripped his elbow tighter.

He looked grim, and that should have warned her away, but Mr. Ingram's claim of poison was fresh in her mind. How easily could someone get poison here in New Orleans? A poison that would mimic a heart attack and eventually kill.

Candlelight guttered when the door opened, setting the shop bell above the door to ringing. The candleflames caught some stray breeze on this windless, humid night. The flames settled when McElroy shut the door.

They paused there, a step into the shop, confined in a short narrow hall, facing a blank wall with a single red-glass sconce. The thick air reeked of incense. Under that was a smothering odor, scents too tangled, too clustered to distinguish. Herbs, fresh and dried. A stinging tincture. Potions distilled or brewing.

She'd visited herbalist shops the world over, and this shop seemed no different—until she spotted the mummified claw dangling from the ceiling, a step into the shop.

Rooster's claw, she guessed, and veered away from walking under it, tugging McElroy to the side.

Like any shop, cases crowded every space to display offered wares. Glass topped some while others were scuffed and scratched wood, stained or worn bare. With the space to walk between the cases so tight and a low ceiling and shadows everywhere, claustrophobia lurked to spring on the susceptible. The windows were even shuttered; nailed shut, she would guess.

A shop like any other, she reminded herself while the dense odor and shadows and claustrophobia preyed on her mind.

Beads clinked as the proprietress came from the back. The woman's hair was a frizzled white halo, her skin wrinkled and as dark as the shadows. Her red dress was the only vibrant thing in the shop. She spoke a Creole patois, some sounds that Nedda understood but wouldn't swear to their meaning.

McElroy understood it. "No gris gris." He shook his head. "A word with the Queen?"

The reply sounded like "*Moun qui la?*" but Nedda was guessing. The woman added, "*La Reina n'est pas là.*"

"I don't believe that." He held up a folded bill, an extraordinary value.

The woman retreated through the beaded curtain. They heard murmurs then a sliding step.

The next woman was tall. Her sculptured face looked like a queen. A garish turban of purple roses, yellow squares, and red squiggles swathed her hair. The shapeless gown was the same fabric. The red lines seemed to writhe in the corners of Nedda's eyes. She stared down her nose at McElroy, of a height with him but seeming taller.

He laid the folded bill on the scratched counter. "Missy has questions."

That stare turned on Nedda. She suddenly wanted to shrink back, but she'd dealt with holy hermits in Arabia and magic practitioners in the Dutch East Indies and shamans in South and Central America. The common behavior in confronting them was never to be intimidated. She lifted her chin. "Do you have a tincture of foxglove? Digitalis? *Digitale?*"

"I know foxglove. You have fast heart?"

"No. A friend. He did have it."

The woman half-shuttered her eyes. "He no more has it."

"Have you sold—?"

She turned on her heel and left through the beaded curtain. She'd never touched the folded money.

The other woman didn't return.

McElroy took her hand. "Come on." He ignored the money. Once paid, it should never be retracted.

"But I want—."

"We've got all the answers we're going to get."

Nedda welcomed the return to humidity without the shop's cloying scents. McElroy guided her past Broussard's, to the corner of the block and beyond before he stopped to hail a taxi. She inhaled deeply, and the balconies and lampposts stopped wavering in her sight.

When he bundled her into the taxi, she tried to peer over his shoulder, looking along the block at a flash of red. "She knows something."

"I'd agree with that, but she won't talk about it."

"With more money—."

"Nope. Not when a death's involved. Don't press it, Nedda."

She should have protested his use of her first name, but the shop odors had given her a headache which swelled to pounding on their return to Roosevelt Hotel.

. ~ . ~ . ~ .

Nedda woke, her slip and body drenched. For a long minute she could not place where she was. Then the purplish shadows streaked with yellow and red dissipated. Her eyes flickered open to sunlight pouring through wispy netting around her bed. A maid folded back the plantation shutters to the balcony, and birdsong trilled joyfully.

Mr. Ingram's funeral was today.

Devensay Four's train would arrive today.

She revived more. Looking around, she saw her Chanel dress draped over a chair, her heels askew on the floor before it.

The maid returned with a pot of strong coffee, a buttery croissant, and fried eggs topped with pink shrimp and a puddle of spicy sauce that a waiter had introduced as cocktail sauce.

"I didn't order this."

"Mr. McElroy." The girl blushed. Hands folded over her crisp white apron, she peeked up then returned her gaze to the floor. "He said you would need it."

"And when did he tell you this?"

"Last night, when I helped him with you. He said you'd had too much wine."

Nedda had never had too much wine in her life, but she didn't argue. Her last minutes of the evening were gone. She remembered reaching the hotel, the wavy shimmer of the brass on the lobby doors, but somewhere between the marble expanse of the lobby and the elevator cage, her memory had faded. "Thank you, Martine. I shall remember your aid to me. Do you know—?" She hesitated, not certain how much the maid knew.

"Mr. McElroy said he would meet you in the garden, about ten o'clock, Miss."

That wasn't what she'd intended to ask, but she was glad to know. "And Mrs. Hyatt Ingram? The new widow? Do you know of her plans?"

"Mr. Clement LaFoy left word that she is to be awakened at eleven this morning. They are to leave for the cathedral at two."

The funeral was set for 2:30 in a side chapel of St. Louis Cathedral. The Anglican Hyatt Ingram would have preferred Trinity Episcopal Church, but Giselle had demanded the service at the cathedral, and LaFoy arranged it for her.

Choosing her battles, Nedda raised no demurral. Neither Colfax nor Sheridan would be present, and Mr. Ingram could no longer care.

She hung up the Chanel dress then had a quick bath before dressing in a black jacket and black long skirt. The ribbon-strap heels would have to serve. She changed to a plain leather envelope clutch, tucking the chandelier earrings in their case and dropping it into the slim purse.

A niggling sense warned her to check the travel case. It was locked, but she still opened it and flipped through the documents and ledger. She slipped the new will and Mr. Ingram's letter into the clutch then locked the case again.

She would have liked to check all the documents and ledgers still with Mr. Ingram's luggage, but Giselle had clearly asked Nedda to leave the suite. She'd not had time to ask when she could arrange his papers. As executrix, she would have to organize them.

But Giselle did not yet know the contents of the new will.

She soon would. Mr. Devensay would ensure that.

4 ~ The Suspects

Few people graced the pews for the funeral. Hyatt Ingram's reputation was London and Arabia. His name had not yet splashed across the United States or Southeast Asia.

The priest performed a standard service, applicable to any stranger. He had kind words to address to the widow, but he stumbled over her name.

Hidden by the wide brim of her black hat, Nedda watched the others gathered to mourn.

The gruff men on the Louisiana Oil board, roughnecks in their youth, had grown up in the petroleum industry. They were uncomfortable in their black suits but owed honor to the London financier who had offered investment, saving their company when gushing oil rigs slowed their output.

Behind the owners and chief officers were younger executives, out to impress their chiefs. They would be newly conscious that most deals happened outside the boardrooms.

A few men were Old South, lucked into the boom. Henderson Beaumont III belonged with them, even though he sat behind the pew reserved for family, a pale woman beside him, her dress and manner proclaiming her the old-moneyed class.

Other wives were scattered among the gruff men, starched and stiff and careful of their husbands' status. A few like Giselle were trophy wives who aped the part but whose glittering jewels and flashes of color bespoke the obvious *nouveau riche* nature of their entry into this close circle. Giselle had chosen cherry pink to offset the funereal black. Her blouse, her heels, ruby and diamond earrings that shouted wealth, the ribbon around the cloche hat that tamed her platinum hair, all set her apart from the muted attire of the status wives.

Clement LaFoy's arm pressed into Giselle's. Nedda couldn't decide into which group LaFoy belonged: Old Money or New Flash. His position with Louisiana Oil remained unclear. He had polish that the other young men lacked, miles ahead of them in the game of Young Executive on the Make, ready to spot a deal. He thought he'd found a new deal, but Hyatt Ingram's new will would change that. He might ride the coaster for a while, but he'd never survive the long climb up the steepest hill.

Was he acting on a double-blind, pretending to focus on Giselle while he actually worked for LOC to prevent Ingram Investments from winning a greater stake in the company?

Hank McElroy had a high executive position with his company Texas P & R. What did he hope to gain? Nedda didn't want to contemplate the greed that drove him.

The parking for the cathedral had filled up with boxy Lincolns and Fords, long Bentleys and Rolls Royces. The driver of their hired automobile, a Markin model, could not find a space near the cathedral. McElroy had the man stop near the cathedral steps. Nedda alighted then watched the cab with its cheery green box drive down the street overshadowed with live oaks and the ubiquitous Spanish moss.

McElroy came in after the service had started, slipping onto the pew beside her.

His tardiness meant he had avoided the maneuvering for the best pews, chiefs and their wives directly behind the family pew, then the young executives. That relegated Nedda to the back. She'd known Hyatt Ingram longer and better than anyone else here, but in the eyes of all, she was a hired employee. Their greetings and platitudes went to the widow.

The priest finished his little sermon for any stranger and the readings from the Psalms. A voice lifted from the choir overhead. The baritone swelled and filled the sanctuary. Nedda stared at the black coffin with its silver medallions, parked in the side aisle, then she studied the painted statue of the cathedral's patron saint. His fingers were lifted in the classic sign of blessing.

Someone coughed. A woman sniffed.

The song ended. The priest read another Psalm.

And Nedda wondered who had poisoned Mr. Ingram. The thought had strayed through her mind several times, yet she hadn't been focused enough to dwell upon it. Too many other things encroached.

Mr. Ingram had said "poison". He'd never had a problem with his health, no matter the heat of Arabia or the soaking monsoons of Asia or other changes of locale or travel.

Poison was readily available and easily found on Bourbon Street. A tourist could buy it from that shop she'd visited. Someone native to New Orleans might have a better source. The key was that anyone could buy a poison.

The question became *Who wanted him dead?*

Giselle? As widow, she inherited a lot of money, even at the reduced level of the new will. Giselle knew Ingram's son would inherit the bulk along with all the shares in the investment company. She didn't have to know about the new will to act against her husband.

Giselle, though, was not the only one who would benefit. Clement LaFoy, current lover, would have his own expectations from the old will. He might think he had enough control over Giselle to command her decisions about her sudden influx of money.

Yet the murder could have nothing to do with the inheritance.

Someone might not have wanted a deeper investment by Ingram into Louisiana Oil. The shares he'd already purchased were a done deal, but the coming vote would lead to a greater investment and more control leaving from the locals to wing across to a London-based financier. They might hope to buy out the widow, not understanding that Giselle would never have a voice in Ingram Investments.

Henderson Beaumont represented LOC. Did he represent men waking late to the realization that they would no longer control their own company if Ingram's greater investment went forward? Beaumont himself had to know that. Had he wanted to stop the buy-in to the company? Had someone who controlled him wanted the vote stopped?

Behind Beaumont sat the accountant Jamison Parker, dressed today in a somber marquise-patterned dark suit, wasp-waisted. The narrow cut of the jacket, lacking the Norfolk belt, suited his slender frame. Slanted pockets and pearlescent buttons that matched his pearl-adorned diagonal tie bar revealed the suit was for fashionable evenings, not a funeral.

Muted flash it was, and that surprised her. She had deemed the accountant for a solemn man, a nervy perfectionist who starched his pocket handkerchiefs into pyramidical points and who straightened the laces on his polished whole-cut Oxford shoes. Previously, he'd dressed in well-tailored suits, allowing a colored tie to provide one touch of a stylish accent. A serious man would never have worn a suit designed for a frivolous occasion to a funeral.

Nedda should have taken better notes when Mr. Ingram was examining the company's ledgers. Jamison Parker hadn't liked the books out of his control for even an hour, but Mr. Ingram had insisted. The money he planned to invest had won that argument. From Parker's anxiety about the books, she might have thought some tallies were hinky, but Mr. Ingram had examined the ledgers. Little had escaped his hawk eyes. Unless the tampering occurred after the books came back. Mr. Ingram had wanted another look, but then he was distracted. He had Nedda copy balance sheets as rapidly as she could while he poured over a prospectus on off-shore drilling.

Off-shore drilling had brought Hank McElroy to Louisiana, to study the water-based rigs in Caddo Lake and the new off-shore rig in the bay. Where did he stand in the vote? She knew Texas P & R had an interest in LOC. The company wasn't a rival, but they wanted a greater share in LOC. Ingram might have blocked that.

Did McElroy commit murder? Were any of them murderers?

Poison was different from a revolver or a knife. It wasn't as personal. Dose a drink and leave, and the murderer didn't have to be present when death occurred.

Beaumont. LaFoy. McElroy. All three equal. All wanted into LOC, a steady oil supply rather than a gusher that would peter out.

She couldn't remember if she had spotted the red door of the voodoo shop or if McElroy had pointed it out or done something to point it out. The evening before was hazy to her. Had he thought it would be a touristy thing to show her, or had he been warning her?

Nedda slid a glance his way and caught his look. He lifted an eyebrow and offered a half-smile.

She quickly looked down. It couldn't be Hank, could it? He was so helpful, so kind, so—handsome. She didn't want the murderer to be him.

His attachment to her might be a ruse, to keep her from pursuing the idea of murder by concentrating on the new will.

Maybe she needed to treat him as an enemy, not as a friend.

The priest began speaking English again, giving the rite of interment. Mr. Ingram wouldn't be buried in New Orleans. The need to be buried aboveground had revolted him. Mr. Chatto had found an inland cemetery. The body would be interred there tomorrow.

Nedda still had that before her.

The priest finished quickly. He came down from the altar to take Giselle's hand and offer a blessing. People began standing, talking. The cloying scent of flowers overwhelmed, and Nedda headed down the side aisle for the entrance where the automobiles waited.

Photographers jostled about as she emerged into sunshine, but she wasn't the widow, and they returned to their talk and smokes.

Hank McElroy appeared beside her. Conscious of her doubts, she edged away, but he stayed with her, even directing her away from the doors as more people flooded out.

She stared at the cemetery beside the cathedral. Spanish moss draped the trees, hanging in straggling clumps, like the witchlocks of old hags, creating a gloomy half-light beneath the oaks. Mr. Ingram deserved to be buried inland, away from this dreary gloom, in the sunshine of a countryside cemetery. He had loved the sunshine of Arabia, soaking up the heat as only someone born and raised in cold England would.

The photographers started shouting, jostling for the best photograph, for Giselle had emerged. Clinging to LaFoy's arm, she enacted the languishing widow, lifting a lace hankie to her eyes. She flashed pretty knees and ankles as she backed into the taxi.

No photographers wasted film on Nedda or McElroy. Henderson Beaumont earned a flashbulb or two. On the steps behind him, Alejandro Chatto would be featured with the influential attorney.

Sheridan Ingram still hadn't contacted her. Colfax hadn't wanted to attend either funeral or interment, and Nedda had no argument to persuade him. At some point he might regret missing this final farewell to his beloved grandfather. He was young, though, and only life had meaning for him.

Hank McElroy walked her to the hired auto, parked around the corner, beneath the heavy crooked branches of a live oak draped in moss. The cemetery's iron-spiked fence squared around the tombs. An angel pointed east, over the edger of oak-stained marble. At their approach, the chauffeur straightened up and threw away his smoke.

"Where next?" McElroy asked. "The hotel?"

"Only briefly. I have to meet Mr. Devensay at the train station. He's arriving on the Crescent at seven o'clock."

"You planning to dine with him?"

"I hadn't really thought."

"We can take him to Broussard's."

She remembered their quiet table in a corner, out of the way and uninterrupted. They had talked the evening away. Then they had ventured into that voodoo shop. Nedda repressed a shudder and concentrated on Hank's plan. "*We* can take him to Broussard's?"

"I'm your guide, aren't I? Smoothing the way at the restaurant?"

"Decidedly true, I must admit." She looked down at the severe suit, black skirt and peplum-skirted jacket, a white blouse with a pleated bodice, all suitable for a sedate dinner. She checked her wristwatch, a flash of silver and gold on the metal band. "We've three hours until the train arrives."

"We can visit a park. Or a gallery."

"I must have my business case when I meet Mr. Devensay."

"Then we'll return to the hotel and get that first." He assisted her into the cab and gave the direction to the chauffeur. Other autos from the funeral passed by slowly, and the chauffeur delayed starting the Markin. McElroy tapped his fingers on the seat before him, watching the long saloons and the boxy sedans rumble past.

. ~ . ~ . ~ .

When Nedda stopped at the hotel desk to retrieve her key, the desk clerk said the manager needed to speak with her. She wondered what the matter was —the charge for her room? Mr. Ingram's documents? Something in the hotel safe?

The clerk returned from the office with the manager. "Miss Courtland, this is fortunate. We have a call waiting for you."

"A call? A telephone call?" Her mind leaped to Colfax Ingram. "Who is it? Is it the Sacred Heart Academy?"

"No, miss. The man gave his name as Sheridan Ingram." Relief flooded her; Sheridan had received her messages. He knew about his father. The manager continued. "Please step over to Box 3, Miss Courtland, and Exchange will connect him."

The hotel had four telephone boxes in the lobby, tucked off to the side, behind the porter's station.

Hank McElroy followed her to the boxes with their gilt numbers and scrolled decorations on the glass surrounding the top half of the box. "Did Ingram know the funeral was today?"

"As soon as I knew, I wired him."

"Then he should have given you time to return from the service. I'll be there." He gestured vaguely toward the seating at the back of the lobby, with its view of the enclosed garden.

She shut herself inside the call box, tapped the line for the operator and identified herself, then waited for Exchange to connect the lines.

It seemed disloyal to agree with McElroy that Sheridan Ingram should have given her time to return from the funeral.

The wait wasn't as long as she expected but longer than she wanted. Mr. Devensay's train would be barreling to them. She didn't want to be late to meet him. Nedda contemplated a half-dozen things to tell Mr. Ingram the younger before the ring came, short and abrupt. She snatched up the earpiece and tiptoed to speak into the mouthpiece. Static crackled. The connection wasn't good. "Hallo?"

"Miss Courtland?" Two words and faint, but she knew the voice. Her heart sank a little, for Sheridan Ingram sounded like his father's. Colfax had that same tone.

Without preamble, she demanded, "Where are you?" She wondered where he had reached on his journey to New Orleans. The vote on the investment was tomorrow afternoon. Even if he arrived late in the morning, she could apprise him of his father's thoughts and decisions.

"In San Francisco."

"But—I hoped you were halfway here. The vote is Tuesday."

"I will not be there. You know my father's plans. You have my power of attorney and my proxy. I can wire a telegram to reinforce that if you wish."

"I do wish it. Why aren't you here?"

"Now, don't worry your pretty little head about that," words he knew would rile her.

"Mr. Devensay will expect you."

He laughed. "That old stump? I'll be glad to miss him."

"Devensay Four."

"Doesn't matter. Four is as bad as Three."

"He will want to deal with you. You're the heir."

"Well, he cannot. I will be in Seattle."

"Seattle? Why—?" She cut off the futile question. The answer wasn't hers to know. Sheridan Ingram still occasionally answered to His Majesty's War Office. She had tried never to pry into that. After they sailed from Hong Kong, he'd told his father that work was off the boil. She wondered if encountering Emerson Werthy in Hawaii had anything to do with this trip to Seattle. "Your father's interment is tomorrow."

"Any uproar about the new will?"

"No. I've kept it quiet. They all assume we're waiting on Mr. Devensay for the reading."

"And that's when?"

"Tomorrow afternoon."

"Anything else, Miss Courtland? I'll be *in communicado* after this. I'm heading for my train."

"Seattle?"

"I said."

"Yes, sir. I mean—Never mind what I mean. Take care, Mr. Ingram. You are all Colfax has. And do not forget that telegram."

"Colfax also has you, Miss Courtland."

"I'm not—."

A decided click and the static ended, and she knew he'd rung off. Still, she tapped the ringer. "Operator? Operator, are you there?"

"Yes, ma'am. How may I assist you?"

"Is it possible to tell me the location for that telephone call?"

"Of course, ma'am." A pause, then the woman returned with "The Fairmount Hotel in San Francisco, California."

"Thank you."

Nedda replaced the earpiece, ending her part of the call. Disappointed, she stood with her hand still on it. She should have expected this turn of events. Sheridan Ingram had been distracted throughout their stay in San Francisco. The day before their departure to New Orleans via Southern Pacific Railroad, he had brought in a lawyer to write the power of attorney and proxy documents. Colfax's enrollment at the Sacred Heart Academy had already been planned. She was to carry it forward.

Now she had the right to act for him in this investment matter.

Mr. Devensay would have much more about which he would not be pleased.

Hank McElroy accompanied her on the elevator to her room. The maid had straightened the room, leaving the balcony curtains wide and returning her suitcase to the wardrobe. She dragged the travel case from the top of the wardrobe and slipped in the documents from her clutch. Then she straightened herself a little, popped a carnation lipstick in her clutch, and hurried out, travel case banging against her knee.

The elevator was slow, stopping at every floor for someone to come on. Crowded against the back wall with McElroy, Nedda tapped her foot and checked her watch.

"We'll get there when we get there," he drawled in her ear.

"He will not be pleased when we are late. Nor that Sheridan Ingram will not appear."

He shrugged. "We have time."

That was Texas, operating on hours and minutes. London time counted minutes and seconds.

They weren't late to the L & N Station, but by some magic Devensay had deboarded, gathered his luggage and a porter, and waited for them at the large clock in the center of the lobby. Nedda cringed when she saw him draw out his pocketwatch and check it against the clock.

Peter Devensay was the fourth generation in the solicitor firm of Devensay, Pethbridge, and Frederick. He had a pinched face, tight chin below thin lips, a long narrow nose, and narrow eyes that barely opened. His dark hair, grey at the temples, was pomaded into strict control. He wore a charcoal suit with a light pinstripe, tailored on Savile Row, and his pocket square still had three starched points. After that hurried train journey, nothing in his appearance or attire showed evidence of the thirteen-hundred miles he'd traveled from New York to New Orleans.

Hyatt Ingram had valued him, and Nedda did as well. As strait and narrow as Peter Devensay was, he had a quick incisive mind and a manner that suffered no fools.

Nedda stopped before him, glad that she had checked her appearance. For anyone trained in the Devensay, Pethbridge mold, a stray curl would be evidence of dereliction of duty, unworthy of a professional private secretary.

"Early," he said. "You surprise me, Miss Courtland."

"Your train must have had a tail wind, to arrive before us." McElroy stuck out his hand. "Hank McElroy, sir, with Texas Petroleum and Refining. Miss Courtland has told me about your firm."

Mr. Devensay lifted one thin eyebrow. She wasn't certain if he disapproved the shortened name or the man. He gave McElroy's hand one shake then drew back. "You have an automobile?"

"We do. It's waiting outside. We thought you might wish for dinner before going to the hotel."

He looked down his nose at Nedda, as if he peered at her through glasses. "I'm amenable to that suggestion. Somewhere quiet?"

"Broussard's Restaurant. You will enjoy it."

He gave her a quick scan, head to toe. "You've come from the funeral."

"Yes, it was this afternoon. The interment is tomorrow. Will you wish to attend that?"

"We shall see." He tipped the porter who had offloaded his suitcase and portmanteau into the back of the Markin. "You will sit in the front, Miss Courtland?"

The question was more like an order. She took the seat beside the driver. Taking a deep breath, she twisted around and plunged in. "We thought we could dine while you perused Mr. Ingram's documents. Somewhere away from the hotel where we can be quiet."

"And uninterrupted by the third Mrs. Ingram," the solicitor noted.

The comment opened a mine field. She didn't know if she should speak openly of Giselle's infidelity; that might paint her jealous of the woman. An employee should not speak slightingly of her employer's family. If she abruptly shared Mr. Ingram's claim of murder, he might think she'd run mad.

She chose safer ground. "You should have time to collect your thoughts, Mr. Devensay. Mr. McElroy chose the restaurant."

On his cue, the Texan described the Commander's Palace, a change from Broussard's that they hadn't discussed. Yet from the dishes and wines he extolled, McElroy must have decided Devensay would enjoy finer flavors.

The restaurant provided them with a quiet corner. The solicitor had mellowed by the time he finished the three courses. Crab croquettes with a remoulade and a creamy soup were followed by a luscious sirloin with a side of braised mushrooms and a bearnaise that made Nedda want to melt.

The waiter tempted them with a special tiramisu. Devensay refused, and Nedda wished he hadn't. She loved tiramisu.

"The documents," he reminded her.

Nedda quickly delved into the travel case for Sheridan Ingram's documents. Devensay merely raised his eyes before he took them, letting them unfold as he drew on wire-rimmed glasses. He read slowly, carefully, and when he looked up, she handed him her copy of Hyatt Ingram's new will and his letter to her.

The waiter came to pour coffee before he looked up from his reading.

McElroy waved him away. "If you will give us a few more minutes," and the waiter backed away.

Devensay returned the papers to their envelopes and handed them back to her. He removed his silver-rimmed glasses and tucked them into an inner jacket pocket. Folding his hands before him, he pinned Nedda with a penetrating gaze. "All is in order. You say the interment is tomorrow?"

"Yes."

"Then we shall miss it, a move I doubt they will expect. You have been spinning your wheels, Miss Courtland. They will continue to think we will not move quickly. We must surprise them."

"I had no instructions, Mr. Devensay."

"You knew Mr. Ingram's wishes, and you have the power of attorney and proxy for Mr. Ingram the younger. That places you in charge of Ingram Investments. I must trust that you will act in obedience to the directives from Mr. Ingram the elder."

"Of course. Yet I can take no action until the reading of the will. That is Monday afternoon."

"And the vote on the investment is Tuesday afternoon? Then in the morning we will acquire the ledgers that Mr. Ingram examined. Our focus will be the company."

He knew nothing of Mr. Ingram's claim of poison. She began haltingly, "Mr. Ingram had good reason for requiring a second will."

"His wife's infidelity."

"Well, yes, but—" She hesitated, yet he had to know everything. "Mr.

Ingram suspected someone had poisoned him. He lost his health so rapidly, and his heart continued to fail. I believe he may have suspected someone in Louisiana Oil."

He didn't shrug, but he came very close to the movement. "Then our quick actions will thwart their plan. They cannot prevent the vote, and you hold the entirety of the Ingram votes based on the proxy."

"Whoever this person is—. I know it's unproveable, but—."

"We shall not hunt into a warren, Miss Courtland. We have no evidence. We will prepare ourselves for the vote. Whoever is the danger will not expect that."

"And the new will? What will you say to Mrs. Ingram?"

He smiled, close-lipped and small, more in his eyes than on his face. "This Mr. Chatto that I have yet to meet must deal with Mrs. Ingram. He oversaw the writing of the will. He is Mr. Ingram's legal representative in that matter. He will oversee your acquiring all you need to execute your duties." He leaned back, and the waiter appeared to pour the coffee. The rich brew didn't reek of chicory, and Nedda thought it just might be drinkable. Mr. Devensay inhaled and smiled. "This restaurant was a fine choice, Mr. McElroy. A worthy end to days of travel." When the waiter stepped away, he leaned over the table and said softly, "Please retain these documents, Miss Courtland. They are extremely important."

She tucked everything into her travel case and buckled it before picking up her coffee.

Yet on the drive to the hotel, with the gentlemen in the back seat and McElroy once more acting as a tourist guide, Nedda slipped them out of the travel case and into her clutch.

5 ~ The Revelation

Nedda dreamed again, a red door and shadows, a croaking raven, silver-rimmed spectacles with a broken lens.

And water dripped on the will, turning the ink into a seeping mess, watery blue ink impossible to read.

She woke, hot and perspiring. She lay still, caught between dream and darkness, staring at the silvered moonlight hazed by the mosquito netting, slanting through the slatted shutters. A faint breeze stirred the netting.

Then a black bulk moved.

Terror froze her to the bed. The dream cracked apart.

The prowler opened the wardrobe and searched. He opened nothing, just flipped through her dresses and pushed her suitcase away.

Then he stepped back and looked up.

Her travel case rested atop the wardrobe. He dragged it down.

He didn't look inside. Clutching the case to his chest, he headed for the door. It opened on oiled hinges. His face was turned away from the hall light. The door shut, and he was gone.

Nedda jumped out of the bed, tangling in the netting in her haste. She stumbled to the door and locked it. She stood there, gasping, holding the key in the lock.

She had locked the door before, and the prowler had still entered.

She brought a chair from the table by the window and jammed it under the door knob. That had been an effective barricade in seedier climes than New Orleans.

Feeling safe, she flicked on the desk lamp.

The prowler had been hunting for her travel case—where she'd previously kept important documents. Not tonight. The only documents it now held were Colfax's enrollment and some correspondence, an old daybook, and an empty ledger.

He had tried to steal the all-important will and letter, the proxy and power of attorney, and the ledger into which she'd copied information from the LOC accounting.

Had he wanted the new will? Only Mr. Devensay, Mr. Chatto, and Hank McElroy knew about that. She suspected the new will wasn't the prowler's focus.

Mr. Ingram's letter to her—several people knew about that. They had seen her read it over and again.

And the proxy and power of attorney for Sheridan Ingram. Giselle knew of those. She'd likely informed Clement LaFoy—and anyone else who would listen to her chatter.

The ledger with the pages of accounts copied from LOC ledgers. Henderson Beaumont knew of that. And Jamison Parker.

She couldn't remember if Hank McElroy knew about the ledger. Devensay Four didn't know.

Whoever the prowler was, they might want the new will to stop her serving as executrix. They would want to destroy the proxy documents to prevent her voting Mr. Ingram's wishes.

She managed only snatches of sleep the rest of the night.

. ~ . ~ . ~ .

Although Mr. Devensay reduced the LOC accounting clerk to jelly, he didn't receive the ledgers he wanted.

"I regret, sir, but it is impossible. When not in the office, Mr. Parker locks the current ledgers in the file cabinet."

All eyes went to the wooden cabinet against the wall behind him, four drawers tall and of honey-colored maple, impressively sturdy.

"This office is open for business today. The ledgers should be accessible," Devensay countered.

"Yes, sir, but I am merely dealing with correspondence and new invoices."

"And where is Mr. Parker?"

"The interment, sir. When he stopped by this morning, he stated he would return this afternoon."

"At what time?"

"He did not specify that, sir."

Nedda couldn't see Devensay Four's face, but at his expression, the clerk hunched his shoulders and looked down. The man hadn't stopped wringing his hands since she had introduced the London solicitor to him. He had seemed competent when she'd come with Mr. Ingram to the office. What about Mr. Devensay had him so perturbed?

She intervened before the man dissolved on the floor. "May we leave a message for Mr. Parker?"

Relief transformed the clerk. "I will see he receives the message immediately upon his return."

He fetched a letterhead sheet and an envelope then tried to hand her a fountain pen. Wary of spurting ink, Nedda used her own fountain pen. Unsurprisingly, Devensay Four dictated the letter, strict sentences that recorded the force of his personality.

When she wrote his name beneath the terse closing, he thrust out his slim, London-pale hand for the pen. He held his glasses to his nose to read then signed.

She wafted the letter to hasten the ink drying before she folded it then wrote Mr. Parker's name across the envelope while Devensay Four stored his glasses in a case. He handed the letter to the clerk. "Give this immediately to Mr. Parker, from your hand to his, as soon as he arrives. You understand the importance and haste."

"Of course, sir."

Hank McElroy and the driver chatted idly as they leaned on the hired Markin. The driver tossed his cigarette and hastened to start the auto while Hank opened the doors for them. He climbed into the front passenger seat then looked around, his eyes meeting Nedda's. "Where next?"

"We've several hours before everyone is expected to Mr. Chatto's office. What would you prefer, Mr. Devensay?"

"I believe I should discover more about the American petroleum industry. The firm handles Mr. Ingram's investments into various endeavors around the world. I confess we had not investigated the American ventures into petroleum."

"Then Mr. McElroy is your man. He represents a Texas firm that is also looking to invest in LOC."

"More like we're looking into off-shore rigs, but yep, I can answer your questions." He said something quietly to the driver, who shifted gears. The vehicle rolled forward as he turned to add, "We can talk over coffee at a restaurant I know, then have lunch there, too."

"A restaurant as fine as the Commander's Palace?"

"Now, that was fine, indeed, but I think you'll like this place, too."

The morning became filled with petroleum, drilling and refining, rigs pumping on land and in the waters of Caddo Lake. With the vote on Tuesday, Nedda listened closely, wanting to learn more before she had to decide to follow Mr. Ingram's original plan or dig in her heels. She would have preferred to hand the vote over to Sheridan Ingram.

Devensay Four asked many shrewd questions, revealing the London firm had not just blindly guarded Ingram Investments. That precise London accent sounded at odds with McElroy's softer Texan drawl, but the two men talked well into lunch and only slowed as coffee was served with a sweet chiffon pie.

Well before anyone else, they arrived at Mr. Chatto's office, and Mr. Devensay drew the New Orleans lawyer into close conversation on wills and Louisiana laws on Probate, called Succession here, widow's portions and executor's obligations. Nedda should have listened, but her ears were tired from the morning. Hank lured her onto the balcony overlooking the garden behind Chatto's office. That temporary respite from duty eased her stress.

Yet the reprieve with birdsong and a tinkling fountain dissipated quickly. Giselle and LaFoy arrived for the reading of the will.

As soon as she spotted Nedda, standing off to the side of Mr. Chatto's desk, Giselle stopped abruptly. Wrapped in a mink stole and strong perfume, she snatched her gloved hand from LaFoy's arm and pointed at Nedda. "Why is she here?"

Mr. Chatto had stood when Giselle entered. "Mrs. Ingram, I do not believe you have met Mr. Peter Devensay, with the London firm Devensay, Pethbridge—."

"I asked why she is here."

He cleared his throat then gestured to the chairs centered before his desk. "If you will be seated, Mrs. Ingram, we may begin."

Clement LaFoy whispered in her ear, but Giselle ignored him. "I object to Miss Courtland's presence. She is a mere employee. Actually, she is no longer an employee. She has no right to be here. And she owes me for the nights she's stayed in that room at the hotel."

Mr. Devensay stepped forward from his corner. "On the contrary, Mrs. Ingram. Miss Courtland has two positions that necessitate her attendance at this reading."

"Two positions?"

"Indeed. She is—."

Giselle talked over his explanation. "Who are you with your fancy talk? You sound English, like my late husband."

"We have not heretofore met. You should have heeded Mr. Chatto's introduction. I am Peter Devensay, a solicitor with the firm of Devensay, Pethbridge, and Frederick in London, England. We dealt with many problems that Mr. Ingram and his company encountered."

She studied him with a slight frown then sniffed. "The London lawyer. My late husband said you wanted to stop his marriage to me. He laughed about it. He chose me over your objections. I'll be laughing when I take his money from you."

"You may find that difficult, Mrs. Ingram."

LaFoy started then peered closer at Devensay Four. "What's this?"

McElroy laughed. He covered it with a cough, drawing the attention of LaFoy and Giselle.

"He has no right—," she started while LaFoy snapped, "Hank McElroy should not be here. He's not in Ingram's will."

"I'm not," McElroy agreed. He straightened away from the mantel. "I will wait downstairs, Chatto. As LaFoy pointed out, I'm not in the will. Since you also aren't, you can join me, LaFoy."

Gisele seized his arm. "I want Clement here. I need his support."

"Then, unless someone else protests, Mr. McElroy may also remain," Mr. Chatto said smoothly. "If you will take your seat, Mrs. Ingram."

She directed LaFoy to the chair beside hers. Once seated, she tossed the mink stole over one shoulder. "Well? Get on with it."

Mr. Chatto resumed his seat. He opened the will and began reading the opening forms.

Giselle again interrupted. "Wait. Shouldn't that London lawyer be reading the will?"

"Certainly not." Devensay had a tight smile. "Mr. Chatto drew up this will for Mr. Ingram last week. He has started filing the Succession with the court."

"A will last week? When did my husband do this?"

McElroy cleared his throat. "I believe you and LaFoy were on an excursion to Grand Isle."

Nedda lifted her gaze from the checkerboard floor, meeting his pale eyes. He smiled, and she returned it. Mr. Ingram knew how to set his trap. Even ill, he ensured everything flowed into the layered steel of the trap. Giselle and LaFoy had talked of the excursion for a solid week. Concerned with Colfax, she hadn't really heeded their conversation. They must have left the same day that she and Colfax had.

"This was after he fell ill?" LaFoy quickly asked.

Chatto opened his mouth. From behind LaFoy, McElroy flashed his hand, and Chatto closed his mouth.

McElroy answered. "You will find the timing close, I'm certain, but we have the evidence of the witnesses. Four, I believe."

"Four, yes," Chatto confirmed.

"The morning you left, Chatto visited and drew up the will by hand, returned to his office to have it typed, then had Ingram sign it in front of his witnesses in the late afternoon."

McElroy was clearly obscuring the dates. The will's dates didn't coincide with what Nedda knew of the dates of Mr. Ingram's illness. He had signed it after he fell ill. She didn't think Chatto would dispute him. And Mr. Ingram himself had ensured no one would dispute the will. She wasn't sure how they had staged it. Maybe Hank McElroy would tell her later.

LaFoy had twisted in his chair to glare at McElroy. "How do you know this?"

"Mr. Ingram sent me for a lawyer."

Then another bit of information snared Nedda. Since Giselle and LaFoy were gone when Mr. Ingram fell ill, they could not have poisoned him.

They could have paid someone to do it. The manservant had seemed enthralled by Giselle. Yet she had dismissed him the moment the mortician took charge of Mr. Ingram's body. Jobless, would he still lie for her?

Had McElroy poisoned Mr. Ingram? How would he benefit? His company was not a rival to Ingram Investments. An infusion of investment cash would benefit Texas P & R as much as LOC would be benefitted.

Mr. Chatto continued reading. The inheritance to the son as heir came first. Sheridan would now have control of the investment company. The substantial bequest to Colfax was not a surprise. The maintenance for Ingram's second wife, living retired in Bath, was no different than the previous will.

Giselle's inheritance was finally reached. When Chatto read her name, she sat straighter and flashed a smug look at LaFoy. Wise in all things monetary, Ingram hadn't written her out of the will; he had bequeathed her a lump sum, seemingly substantial. When first she'd read this new will, Nedda had done a rapid calculation. That total amount did not approach the three years' maintenance for Lady Clare, not counting her shares in Ingram Investments.

But Giselle wouldn't know that.

She looked vastly pleased at the lump sum. She scowled at Ingram's insult about her paramour. "How dare--! Well—." She huffed. "It doesn't really matter. He can't control what I do with my money. Not now. Isn't that right, Clement?"

LaFoy didn't answer her. He was running numbers, matching them mentally to Lady Clare's bequest. He also didn't know about the shares in Ingram Investments.

Chatto continued, heading into Nedda's role as executrix and her requirement to remember the bequests of the previous will.

Then came Ingram's threat: any opposition to this will, and the executrix had the power to nullify any noted bequest.

Nedda didn't think a court would let the threat stand … but courts were a gamble.

Mr. Chatto finished and folded the will.

Devensay Four stepped into the light. "There we have it. Our respective roles assigned to us."

"Finally." Giselle popped up. The mink slipped, and she flipped the end once more over her shoulder. Perfume wafted out. "Come, Clement. I want to celebrate. We must go to Bourbon Street."

LaFoy was starting to look ill at ease. "I have a few questions—."

McElroy's rumble silenced LaFoy. "The will is very straightforward. And not to be questioned, or Mrs. Ingram will lose her inheritance."

"That will not happen. Come on, Clement." She rushed out, ignoring Nedda and Devensay Four. He followed, with a lowering brow that foretold he would soon understand just what Hyatt Ingram had managed.

Devensay Four shut the door as they left the anteroom for the stairs. He rubbed his hands together. "Having an investigator's report on Giselle Hampton, I anticipated a bit more trouble from her. Ingram knew her, though. She won't risk a lump sum."

"But it's nothing to Lady Clare—."

His quick glance silenced Nedda. "Giselle Hampton and her paramour have no idea of everything coming to Lady Clare. Shall we return to the hotel and peruse those ledgers that Mr. Parker will have brought?"

But those ledgers had never arrived.

Nor had Mr. Parker.

And the accountant had sent no reason for his absence.

By then, the hour was past six o'clock. Offices would be closed, and even a peremptory message from London's keenest solicitor would not free the ledgers from their locked drawers.

Nedda would not have been Jamison Parker for anything. Devensay Four's wrath would fall in the morning.

She did, however, greatly enjoy her dinner with Hank McElroy at Broussard's again.

. ~ . ~ . ~ .

No one disrupted Nedda's sleep, but they would have had a difficult time with a silent bypass of her safeguards. She blocked the hallway door with the straight-backed chair and sacrificed a Chinese silk scarf to tie together the narrow doors to the balcony.

Although he had arranged to meet at breakfast, Devensay Four never arrived.

Nedda felt mean for enjoying her strong tea and boiled egg and pastry in peace. Her foldover clutch rested on her lap, stuffed with the all-important papers and her ledger.

Hank McElroy sailed in as she sipped the last of her tea. He lowered his lanky frame into the chair catercornered to hers. "You look refreshed."

"Did I look so haggard last evening?" At his consternation, Nedda bubbled with laughter. "I did not think you would be so easy to tease."

His pale eyes brightened, and that slow smile she liked transformed his strongly-boned face. "I expected you to be Miss Serious this morning. Devensay not yet down?"

"No, which is unexpected. All the solicitors in that firm are quite punctual."

"We best roust him out then."

McElroy knocked hard on Devensay's door. "Do you think that's quite hard enough?" she teased.

A passing man grunted. "Hard enough to wake the dead. I need my coffee."

At his words, McElroy knocked harder, and Nedda became concerned. She looked for the floor steward.

He appeared when McElroy knocked a third time. "Open the door," the Texan demanded.

The steward hesitated.

"Please," Nedda asked. "Mr. Devensay was supposed to meet me for breakfast over an hour ago. He didn't come down. I fear he may have fallen ill. He's from England, you know."

The added information spurred the steward to draw out a key, attached to him by a long fob chain. He unlocked the door with the master then stood back.

McElroy started in then backed out. "Get Mr. Vaccaro, man. And a doctor. And the police."

"What—?" The man glanced in then bolted to obey.

Nedda tried to see in, but he blocked her view. "You don't need to see that."

She saw legs on the floor, clad in dark pinstripe trousers and Oxford shoes polished to a high gloss. He lay partly on the faded Oriental carpet, partly on the oak flooring. A dark stain had spread over the carpet.

Nedda backed away, not anxious to see more. Her friend Isabella Tarrant had long ago shared that seeing the victim was the hardest thing to drive from her thoughts.

A bluff former policeman arrived, hotel security. Nedda often spotted him in the lobby, trying to look unobtrusive. Felix Vaccaro, one of the hotel owners, came in the next elevator. Mr. Devensay's death appalled the man. A jangling siren announced the police would soon arrive, but a doctor came next, to pronounce the obvious.

The police ushered Nedda and Hank McElroy away from the scene. Mr. Vaccaro offered an empty office. A young policeman, very stiff in his uniform, stood guard inside the office door. He didn't want them to talk.

Hands shoved deep into his trouser pockets, McElroy paced. Nedda remained in a hard chair at the table, swinging her leg in time with his pacing.

A plainclothes detective arrived. Nedda checked her watch. An hour seemed to have passed, but it was only fifteen minutes.

The detective, who introduced himself only as Mazante, knew about Mr. Ingram's death and funeral and the will reading yesterday. He didn't know that the all-important LOC ledgers were to be hand-delivered this morning by Jamison Parker, directly into Peter Devensay's hand.

His heavy eyebrows raised. He stroked his shaved chin. "And you haven't seen Parker this morning?"

Nedda shook her head. "I didn't, but he could have come before I went to breakfast. Were there ledgers in Mr. Devensay's room?"

McElroy huffed with impatience. He rested a light hand on her shoulder. "Have you asked the desk clerks? In the past weeks, Parker has visited here often enough that they should know him. Did you ask them?"

The detective didn't answer either of them. "Miss Courtland, would you tell me the reason this Mr. Devensay came to New Orleans?"

"His firm acts for Mr. Ingram and for Ingram Investments, in London. On Mr. Ingram's death, he came at the behest of the firm, to look into the business affairs."

"He couldn't have arrived from London? Not that quickly?"

"No. He was already in New York. He arrived Sunday afternoon on the Crescent."

He checked his notebook. "I was given to understand that Alejandro Chatto was Mr. Ingram's attorney."

"Mr. Chatto drew up Mr. Ingram's new will. He's overseeing Probate, which I believe you call Succession here in Louisiana, Mr. Mazante."

"That's correct, Miss Courtland. Succession. I understand you're the executrix for Mr. Ingram's new will."

"Yes."

"And she has the heir's voting proxy for the investment company," McElroy inserted.

"Do you indeed? What did the widow think of that?"

"I wouldn't know, sir."

"What did the widow think of Mr. Devensay?"

Nedda shrugged. McElroy snorted. "Neither she nor her paramour Clement LaFoy had any thought to give to Devensay, not once they knew Chatto drew up the will and Miss Courtland would execute it."

"Paramour, um? It lies that way?"

"It does."

Det. Mazante wrote in his notebook.

"Look," McElroy said. "You need to think who would want Mr. Devensay dead. The reason for the murder?"

His dark eyes shifted between them. "And who would want a London lawyer dead?"

"Tell him, Nedda."

The detective glanced between them then focused on her. "You knew Mr. Devensay before Sunday?"

"As I said, his firm acted for Mr. Ingram, and I was private secretary to Mr. Ingram for over a decade." Her eyes unexpectedly filled. She blinked rapidly to fight the tears. He waited through her faltering. "This afternoon, the owners and chief officers of Louisiana Oil will vote on investments that constitute a buy-in to the company. Mr. Ingram had an initial buy-in some months ago; he hoped to increase his ownership in the company. Mr. McElroy represents Texas P & R—."

"Petroleum and Refining," he clarified.

"Which also wants to buy into LOC. Mr. Devensay intended to review the current ledgers to ensure all accounts remained the same. Yesterday morning he asked to see the ledgers. They were not available for review, for Mr. Parker had them locked away. Mr. Parker was to deliver them early yesterday afternoon—but he failed to do so. Then he was to bring them, a hand delivery by him to Mr. Devensay. That was to happen the first thing this morning."

"How might the accounts have changed?"

She'd thrown a lot of information at Det. Mazante. She didn't know if he'd caught all of the salient details. "I do not know," she said patiently. "Mr. Ingram reviewed the ledgers a fortnight ago, at which time I copied down the last few pages of the balance sheets. Mr. Devensay may have believed changes might have happened after Mr. Ingram returned the ledgers."

"When did Ingram return the ledgers? What's this 'fortnight'?"

"Two weeks. I have my ledger here." She touched her clutch, bulky with everything it held. She drew out the ledger and flipped it to display the running columns of numbers she'd transcribed. "Mr. Ingram himself may have asked to see the accounts before the vote. He was scrupulous about finances."

"Would that be expected? That he would check again?"

"Yes. He died before that could happen. As Mr. Devensay has."

"Very conveniently for the murderer, don't you think?" McElroy asked. "Look, Parker failed to produce the ledgers all day yesterday. They're not here now."

"How do you know that?"

"You didn't say they were."

"He promised to deliver them," Nedda added quietly. "Why wouldn't the ledgers be here, if he had delivered them as promised?"

McElroy straightened and crossed his arms, boss of the oil field. "We need to talk to Parker. And look at those ledgers he keeps locked away."

Mazante stood. He flipped his notebook closed and slipped it into an inner pocket in his loose jacket. "I agree with you. Coming, Miss Courtland?"

A church clock tolled off the noon hour when the patrol car lurched to a stop at the LOC offices. A man was inserting a key into the door when the detective reached him. He dropped a hand on the man's shoulder.

The man jerked around, and Nedda recognized the accounting clerk who'd given no aid to Mr. Devensay.

"Locking the office?" she asked before Det. Mazante spoke. "I wouldn't. These men are with the New Orleans police. They wish to speak with Mr. Parker."

"Is he in?" The detective had produced a wallet and flashed his badge. The clerk swallowed. "He's in."

"He sent you away? Is he planning to destroy the ledgers?" McElroy opened the door and strode inside. Nedda followed, ahead of Mazante, who had to turn the clerk over to the patrolman who'd driven here.

McElroy headed straight for the accountant's office. Nedda and Mazante stayed with him. He pushed open the door, revealing Jamison Parker behind his desk, an open case before him, into which he tried to jam a ledger. The yellow-striped blue plaid of his Norfolk jacket stood out against the dark bookcase behind him. His hair was ruffled, and his tie was missing. The blue plaid didn't match his gray trousers.

"Drop that," Mazante ordered. "Miss Courtland, do you have your copy of the ledger?"

"Her copy?" Parker squeaked.

"Indeed I do, but—why do you have on a sporting jacket, Mr. Parker? I understood LOC to be strict about employee attire in the office.

Where is your suitcoat?"

McElroy chuckled. "Good catch, Nedda. Gray, wouldn't it be, Parker?" He reached behind the door and brought out a suit jacket that matched Parker's trousers. He flicked up the right sleeve. A dark stain covered the cuff. "Evidence, Det. Mazante?"

Parker tried to leap around the desk. The big detective grappled with him then bent him over the desk. The open case toppled to the floor, and two ledgers slid with it, clunking on the oiled wood. "McElroy, if you would send the officer to me."

The accountant groaned.

. ~ . ~ . ~ .

With the LOC company accountant in jail, charged with murder, the investment vote had to be delayed.

Within the month, company officers discovered irregularities in the accounting ledgers, a recent embezzlement masked by double books.

Nedda would have flung everything away to cast the double stains of murder far from her.

Yet Colfax was thriving at the Academy. Although Sheridan hadn't re-contacted her, Devensay, Pethbridge, and Frederick claimed she was the best person to understand the investments Mr. Ingram had planned.

Privately, she thought the solicitors didn't want to sully their hands with LOC and the stained threads tangled around the investment.

Life became easier when Giselle left with Clement LaFoy for New York City, taking the Crescent train north to receive her lump sum from a bank allied with the venerable Bank of England.

Hank McElroy was doing everything in his power to keep her in New Orleans, wining and dining at the best restaurants when she would go and al fresco picnics when she would not. He coaxed her into dancing in the Blue Room at the Roosevelt and attended services with her at Trinity Episcopal.

"Although I'm Methodist," he twinkled as they enjoyed morning tea and coffee at a Vieux Carré restaurant with tables in the garden. A breeze drifted through, stirring the riotous flower blooms and swaying the dangling Spanish moss in the green-leafed oaks. A gnatcatcher swooped in to land on a thick clump, pecking at insects. Then he sobered and gestured at the letter in her hand, emblazoned with the LOC crest. "Is that notice of the next investment vote?"

"It is. You should have received a similar letter."

"I expect it was sent to the company office. They'll send a telegram with the date and time I need to be there."

"The tenth at 10 a.m."

"Easy enough to remember." He peered over the rim of his coffee. "And what will you do after? You have Ingram Investments to manage.

Do you travel to London?"

She turned her teacup on its saucer. "My long distance contact with Devensay, Pethbridge is working well. Until his father arrives, if ever he does, I do not want to leave Colfax entirely on his own. His father did ring him last week, but their conversation was brief. Sheridan Ingram is still half the continent away."

"You'll stay longer, then. But not here in New Orleans. The city is no place to be in summer."

She leaned back, leaving an arm extended to the table so she could idly turn her empty teacup. "Do you have a suggestion?"

"Come to Texas. Devensay, Pethbridge can contact you just as easily there as here. Colfax will be only a telephone call away. Your business with LOC means you now have business with Texas P & R. Time you met more roughnecks than me."

"Will I like them as much?" she asked lightly.

He grinned, eyes sparkling, always a sign of happiness. "Not as much. I'm still running first."

A little thrill ran through Nedda as she chuckled.

That night, she drew out her Pitman Daybook. She hadn't opened it since Mr. Ingram's death. She flipped through the pages, remembering the old man, their working companionship, the places they had traveled.

She reached the listing of addresses. One name caught her eye. Her last letter to Isabella Tarrant was before Christmas. Now spring blossomed everywhere. Time for another letter.

"Dear Isabella," she wrote, smiling to herself, "I have solved a mystery, and I must tell you about it. And about a tall Texan named Hank McElroy. I think you'd approve."

. ~ . ~ . ~ . ~ . ~ .

TEXAS
Sun

COURTING TROUBLE BOOK 2

M. A. LEE

Texas Sun

1 ~ Means

The morning blasted, bright white.

Colfax Ingram grabbed Nedda's arm and jerked her behind the cab of the big Army truck as a second explosion shuddered the oil patch.

Shouts erupted. Debris rained onto the steel truck hood. She cowered against the mud-caked wheel as pings and clangs and clunks broke over them. Colfax crouched beside her until the debris stopped pinging on the Liberty truck. Then he leaped to his feet and ran toward the yelling men.

Nedda straightened and braced a hand on the steel heated by the Texas sun. She dreaded looking toward the drilling floor.

Her tall Texan, closer to the explosion and danger, remained upright.

The oil derrick remained erect, ninety feet into the blue sky, not yet hazed with summer heat. Leroy clung to the top and shouted down.

Her Hank deflected questions from Denny, the youngest roustabout. Colfax loped toward them.

The motorman Fuller levered up from the engine. He had flung himself across the equipment that ran the bit chipping deep into the ground. Centered under the derrick, O'Hara swung a chain to release it from the pipe.

Beyond the planked drilling platform, the job foreman Rhode Tabbert and the driller Witt straightened from their crouch. They'd been shack-side of the platform, closest to the explosion, and the shockwave had rolled over them first. Tab brushed dirt from his shoulders. Witt spat on the ground then peered at the derrick's top. He gestured at Leroy then turned back to Tab.

Heart beating again, Nedda looked for the explosion's cause.

Splintered planks, twisted pipes, and warped tin littered the ground beyond the derrick, flung outward from a churned-up crater in the desert floor. The tool shack had disappeared.

She came around the Liberty's front and perched on the heavy steel bumper. Her movement caught Hank's attention. He tapped his head then pointed at her. She sighed then fetched his battered hat from the cab and crammed it on her head. Then she picked her way to the derrick, watching the ground to avoid curled pieces of knife-sharp tin and shards of splintered wood.

The explosion had catapulted the drilling pipes stacked beside the tool shack. Twisted and bent, they littered the desert. None had landed near the truck.

As she approached, Leroy began his climb down. At 90 feet in the air, he more than doubled the distance from the truck to the destroyed shack, but he reached the drilling platform before she reached Hank and the others.

She stepped over a twisted and torn pipe, unusable. The drilling would have to stop now.

Hank McElroy shouted at the motorman. Fuller bent to the engine. It sputtered to a stop, leaving a strange silence.

Broken by raised voices. Tab and Witt, arguing. Again.

Nedda reached the men. Without looking, Hank stretched back his hand. She took it, and he drew her to his side.

Colfax started around the drilling platform.

"Stop, boy," O'Hara snapped.

He stopped, but the twitch of his shoulders expressed disagreement. "The danger is over."

"Let O'Hara go first," Hank said.

"I'll go with you." Of an age with Colfax, Denny had revived with the excitement.

"Ain't no reason," O'Hara groused. "Ain't nothing left." They all looked at the cratered epicenter of the explosion.

Fuller wiped his hands on a greasy rag. "No more drillin' without new pipe." He nudged a warped pipe with his boot. "Can't use nothin' of what we had."

"When does the next train run?" Hank asked, a question Tab should answer, but he was ensnarled in another argument with Witt.

None of the roustabouts looked at the two men who had charge of the oil patch. "Thursday," Fuller said.

Hank wiped the sweat trickling down his temple. He gave a short nod, moving ahead without Tab and Witt. "I'll telephone the office to send a shipment."

"You do that." The motorman rubbed his stubbly jaw as he looked over the debris field. "I guess we'll clean up the mess."

Denny groaned.

"I'll be back to help after I contact the office." Hank turned toward the truck.

"Wait." Nedda dragged down his hand and dug her brogans into the sand of the desert. "What caused the explosion?"

Hank stopped. He gave no sign of the need for haste, only a willingness to accept her question as necessary. In the three weeks since they'd met in New Orleans, not once had he slighted her input, treating her like a partner as well as a beloved, a courtship that she preferred over flowery words.

O'Hara sighed heavily. He wiped his brow then re-settled his hat. "Might've been me. Weren't no problems with the refining barrels this morning, but I might should've checked it closer."

"How much oil had you refined?"

"Enough to run the engine for a week. The diesel we had were running low."

"That'd account for the second explosion," Fuller mused.

"Yep."

"Then what the f—beggin' yer pardon, ma'am." Denny flushed under his work grime. The bruising sliding under his right eye flared purple. "What the heck caused the first explosion?"

"What indeed?" Hank sounded grim.

He had a right to be grim. The oil patch was nearly a year beyond the predicted two years of drilling. In the last few months one problem after another had plagued the roustabouts, troubles enough that Texas Petroleum and Refining had first sent Rhode Tabbert as foreman to speed up drilling and then sent Hank to determine if the patch was worth further investment.

And Hank had asked Nedda to accompany him. Curious about field drilling and pleased at his invitation, she accepted. Colfax came with her, off for the summer months from the Sacred Heart Academy.

"Tab, get over here," Hank shouted.

The argument stopped.

The foreman came, trailed by the driller who ran the oil patch.

Nedda hadn't determined the problem between the two men. Tab had a forceful personality and snapped his orders, but he worked alongside the men. He didn't have the experience of Witt and O'Hara, but he knew engines and stringing pipe as well as Fuller. Witt's nasal twang edged across bone, but he'd grown up drilling oil. What he didn't know wasn't worth knowing. He didn't lay about with his orders. Tab irked the man, and Witt didn't let a day pass without a handful of arguments.

She glanced around the gathered men. Luck had saved them from injury, but the explosion could have seriously harmed one or more of them.

Or killed one of them.

Cold ran over her, dissipating the summer heat.

While Hank spoke with Tab and the roustabouts, she turned to Colfax. "Are you coming to town?"

"I'll stay here. Give them a hand with clean-up." He grinned, a sudden shift of his oft-solemn face. His grey eyes had a curious gleam. "Maybe find out how crude oil is turned into diesel."

"You do that."

He gave an abrupt nod then turned away, punching Denny high on his arm. The two trotted away to gather ruined pipes.

Hank caught her hand. "We're going."

When her tall Texan moved, he dropped that slow drawl and went. She had to lengthen her stride to keep up.

Tab's presence at the truck surprised her, but it made sense. The foreman would know the number of supplies the office would need to replace.

Hank boosted her to the driver's seat and climbed up as she slid to the middle. Tab waited at the grill to prime the engine. He stared at the oil patch.

Hank fiddled with the gears. "Crank it."

Tab gave three hard, fast turns. The Liberty's engine sputtered then caught with a revving roar. As he came around the engine cab, Nedda opened the passenger door. He climbed in as the big motor sputtered then settled into a muted roar.

Hank leaned forward and unclamped the wind shield. He motioned, and Tab copied him. With the glass down, the wind from their movement would cool the building heat.

"What was it this time?"

Tab grunted. "Same old, same old."

Nedda caught a breath, but Hank said nothing. He turned the army truck in a tight circle then headed for the track that aimed for the town. The Liberty bounced over rocks, jostling them on the hard seat. She leaned into Hank to avoid bumping Tab. The breeze tugged at her hat, and she dragged it off her head to hold in her lap.

Hank didn't wait long. "Tell me." He raised his voice over the motor and wind. "Or is he still on about giving Stevie's money back?"

"That, too."

"What's first?"

Tab watched the scrub of the passing desert, wattle and mesquite, the tall blooms of agave cactus and clumps of creosote brush. A tall bird streaked from under a mesquite and ran across the track to disappear in burnt red rocks. "Witt thinks we're drilling in the wrong place."

"*Now* he agrees with you? Nearly three on this patch, he's argued that there's oil in the hole, and *now* he decides you're right?"

"We're not as deep as we could be. We've had bad luck. Drill bit broken. Engine giving out or blown to bits. Pipes the wrong size. Other patches aren't having these problems. We should strike soon."

"Tab, what are you saying?" Hank shifted gears as the truck labored up a rise. "Now *you* think there's oil here?"

Tab compressed his lips and looked back at the desert. "I think it interesting that Witt wants to find another patch on the same day that the shack exploded."

"Sabotage?!"

Tab shrugged. "It's a dirty word, but it fits."

"Witt has brought in wells for us before."

"I'm not accusing. Maybe it is coincidence."

"You think Witt and O'Hara——."

"I don't know what to think, and that's truth, Mac. My gut's telling me, told me all morning, that we're close. It's deep and massive, and we just need faith."

"Your gut's telling you to keep the faith?"

Tab huffed a laugh. "Yep, exactly that. And for you to use the `phone at Doc Turner's."

"Not the depot?"

"Nor the grocer's," Nedda added, naming the most public of the three telephones in town.

She said nothing about the explosion. She kept quiet whenever Hank talked with Tab about the oil business. Conversation about Texas P & R didn't concern her. She did question whatever affected Ingram & Son Investments, for she had responsibility and interest in that company. In her travels with her late employer Hyatt Ingram, she'd gleaned information about leases and mineral rights and contracts. She knew finances and the business side of petroleum. High up in Texas P & R, Hank knew both sides of the oil industry.

Convinced of oil in west Texas, Texas P & R used science and common sense to sink three wells in the vastness of Hartman County. The first well, close to the town clustered around the depot, had come in with a gush and enough oil to pay for its investment. It ran slow, though, and sputtered, promising a bust rather than a boom. Buzzard No. 2, dry for two years, was abandoned to throw all efforts at the third site. Buzzard No. 3 gave just enough oil to promise more further down.

If Buzzard No. 3 came in, it would be the first benefit the town had seen since its founding in the far-off dry past of the Chichuahuan desert. The land didn't welcome them, producing nothing in soil baked by a blazing sun into dry rock and sand. The people depended on trucked-in food to survive. Only nocturnal animals and spiny or thorny plants thrived in Hartman County.

At Nedda's warning about the gossip that spread when people overheard telephone conversations, Hank swore.

The Liberty truck jerked over a rock and ground to the top of the rise, offering a wider view of the desert.

He leaned forward, glaring at Tab. "What was the argument this morning?"

"Witt wants to move a mile to the south."

"We don't have a mineral rights agreement one mile to the south."

"No, we don't. And we're not likely to get it. At least, I'm not. Land's owned by Collier."

"The railroad clerk?"

Nedda's wince echoed Hank's. Mr. Collier worked for the railroad. A lonely man with a lonely occupation, time had aged him early. He remained protective of the people in "my town". When Hank had arrived, Mr. Collier approached him with complaints that the people who'd signed leases to Texas P & R had been duped.

"We can offer him an improved lease."

"He won't sign it." Tab sounded sure, his gaze on a trail of Texas longhorns maneuvering through a thicket of mesquite. "He's not an easy one to talk to."

"If the oil comes in," Nedda said quietly, "he'll be a wealthy man. Have you pointed that out? It would matter to some."

"Don't see it mattering to Collier," Hank rebutted. "He likes being cranky and lonely."

She glanced at Hank. How had he missed—? She shook her head. Sometimes men missed the obvious. "He's in love with Millie Donovan."

"So?"

"She's in love with the idea of leaving Hartman County. She knows an oil man will eventually leave a no-name town and take his new wife with him. Out of here. Gone for good."

Hank paused the truck to pick the track down the rise. "Explain to a blind man, please."

"Tab's an oil man."

Beside her, Tab stiffened. Hank looked around her at the foreman. "I haven't seen you with Millie."

Tab kept watching the cattle. "No, that's over."

Three words, but they confirmed what Nedda had guessed after a single evening of watching the young beauty interact with the oil men. Millie had ignored Tab the entire evening.

Hank looked confused. "She flirts with Denny."

"That's not serious. Denny isn't important to her. He's too young."

Tab grunted. "She didn't stop her brother when Stevie punched Denny."

"Exactly. She didn't care. She has her sights set on Leroy or Fuller. I haven't decided which one. She may not have decided." Tab shifted, uncomfortable with Nedda's insights. She continued, undeterred. "Leroy might be more impressionable, but he's a stubborn streak. Fuller's steady. Or maybe she wants to make Mr. Tabbert jealous."

Very carefully, Tab leaned away from her, pressing against the truck door as if she were a sybil to avoid.

"Witt would see all of that," Nedda added, more certain now, "especially since he watches everything after he leaves the poker game. He sees how Millie serves Mr. Green without interacting with him, that she blushes whenever Mr. Collier compliments her, that she tries to coax Stevie not to risk so much during the game. She teases Denny, and she flutters her eyelashes at Fuller and Leroy. And Witt watches all of you."

"Trouble all around," Hank said and started the truck down the rise.

The big Liberty jolted and slipped over rocks, but gradually it crept closer to the distant cluster of buildings that formed the no-name town around the Hartman County railroad depot.

2 ~ Motive

Nedda slid down from the truck's bench seat onto the sandy dirt. Hank steadied her.

She snatched off the hat and tiptoed to plant it on his head.

"Hey now." He reached to remove it. "I told you the Texas sun is hotter than you realize."

She blocked his hand. "And I told you that I've traveled the deserts of Arabia. It's the same sun and the same heat and the same kind of desert."

"Not quite the same," but he stopped reaching for the hat. He dug into his trouser pocket and produced his room key. He bent closer. "The attaché in my room. Have a look over the license agreements for me. I think I brought a map of the county."

"I don't imagine that map has much detail. The cattle outnumber the people, 400 to 40. Are you planning to visit the depot?"

"Maybe this evening."

She reached into her purse and retrieved his wallet, her first chance to restore it to him. His brow arched. "You dropped it this morning."

He tucked the wallet into his back pocket, not mentioning his early morning visit, to talk over plans for the day and indulge in a few kisses. His gaze caught the glinting heat of those kisses, and Nedda melted. She swayed.

"Stop your love-making," Tab growled. "We need to get the supplies back to the patch."

She blinked at reality's intrusion. "You need a button on that back pocket."

"Doubt I'd use it." Hank traced a work-roughened finger over her cheek. "My fair English flower is a little sun-burned."

"I'll buy a hat. You keep yours."

"Do that." He pressed a quick kiss to her lips. She stepped back, and he swung up to the driver's seat. The idling engine gave a muted roar. Tab must have spoken, for he looked at the man then back down at her. "Remember," he mouthed.

He wasn't talking about the hat.

She stepped further back. The Liberty truck lurched into movement, heading for Doc Turner's office cum house on the edge of town.

Save for the truck, the street remained empty, but people lived inside the heat-sapped buildings. The town had entered the quiet snail's pace of a summer morning.

She waved the stirred dust away then crossed to the saloon, an older building that had its heyday decades ago, when cattle drivers had to pass through Hartman County on the quickest passage to the railroad. The railroad powers had eventually laid a spur line through the county, only a few years before the massive drives ended.

Colfax had drunk up the information regaled to him by Mike Donovan, the saloon and hotel owner, on their first night in town. His wife Louisa served them a spicy supper that she expected the newcomers to reject. Nedda and Colfax had encountered Kerala and Masala curries in India and Sichuan hot pots and rice noodles in Hong Kong. Colfax had shocked the woman when he asked for more.

The Donovans' daughter Millie hadn't appeared that first night, but she hadn't neglected them since. Her chatter often enlivened the evening meal. Nedda supposed it wasn't the beauty's fault that every man who encountered her looked thunder-struck for the next hour. Millie had probably thought she'd hooked Tab. Yet he slipped away.

Why had Tab wriggled off that hook?

Mr. Collier was certainly still caught.

And Witt?

When Hank had coaxed her to come on this trip, she told him her primary reason was to quench her curiosity about west Texas. That was burned out by a third day of scant water and melting heat. Her real reason was to explore their attraction, deepened by his support following the murder of her late employer Hyatt Ingram. As different as their backgrounds were, they shared the same values and morals.

At the back of her mind was a ticking clock. Ingram & Son Investments still employed her, and soon Sheridan Ingram would conclude his venture in the Pacific Northwest, arriving in New Orleans without notice. He would scoop up Colfax and demand she drop everything to return to London. If Hank McElroy was intended for her, she had to discover that now. A relationship conducted through correspondence would suit neither of them.

The romance was there. The compatibility was. Would both lead to more?

Mindful of her mission, Nedda entered the dim saloon. The mid-morning sun didn't penetrate the windows shaded by the wide balconies off three sides of the first floor. Without the bustle of husband and wife, daughter and two sons, the big room displayed its weary age in spur-gouged planks, scuffed tables and floors, and weathered paints. The customers had vanished, gone to the day's work. Faintly came occasional voices and the clatter of pots from the kitchen.

She climbed the stairs, leaving behind the shadowy cool below. The windows at either end of the long hall stood open, and bright light flooded in, bringing with it the building heat, unstirred by any wind. Her room was to the left, in the northeast corner, a room that didn't gain the afternoon heat of the westward side.

Tab had given up the largest room for her and crowded in with Denny, casting the youth into a narrow cot. Hank had taken the sole empty room, sharing it with Colfax who slept on another scrounged army cot. Fuller and Leroy had the room with bunkbeds, narrow and tight. Witt and O'Hara had the narrow rooms in the middle, across from the stairs and the bathing room.

Hank's door stood open.

Nedda gripped his key tightly so it wouldn't jingle. She didn't creep, but the faded carpet runner still muffled her steps. His room was across from hers, and on many mornings they opened their doors at the same time.

And closed them at the same time.

She didn't know whom she expected. Stevie Donovan was a shock.

He bent over Hank's bed, the attaché open and papers strewn across the patchwork quilt.

Nedda folded her arms and leaned against the door jamb. "Good morning, Stevie."

He jerked. The color ran high on his freckled cheeks when he looked her way, only traces of his beautiful sister on his face. He dropped the papers.

"May I help you find something? Contracts and lease agreements are dry reading."

"I did not—I was not—Miss Courtland, I didn't expect you. Didn't you go to the work?"

"Indeed, we left incredibly early, at dawn. Unfortunately, we had an explosion at the oil patch."

"An explosion? Of the drilling equipment? It's gone?"

"No."

He winced.

Now why would he wince?

"You left your snooping a little too long."

"Snooping? I wasn't snooping."

"Yes, you were. You're sticking your nose where it does not belong." Then she said the fatal slight for a teenager who wanted to be a man. "Does your father know what you are doing?"

He flew into anger, cursing her in a mix of English and Spanish. She didn't understand most of his words. *Basta* she understood, but Spanish wasn't one of her languages. From his vehemence, with the *vete a la chingada*, Nedda didn't want the translation. She stepped aside as he barreled toward the door and watched him run for the stairs.

An extreme reaction, but teenagers could be extreme. Was it embarrassment at being caught snooping? Or something more sinister? Theft? Spying?

Why would anyone need to spy?

Then she remembered the sabotage.

Nedda had sorted the documents and restored them to the attaché before another sound came from the hall. She refused to look around. She took her time closing the satchel and buckling it.

The person cleared their throat.

She looked around then. Millie's luxurious hair was tamed under a kerchief. Color stained her cheeks, and her scowl reminded Nedda of the fish wife of nursery tales.

"Oh. Hi." The shorter greeting was friendlier. "Did Stevie send you?"

"He did. Miss Courtland, I do apologize. Stevie—."

"I'm the wrong person. Stevie should apologize to Mr. McElroy. These are his documents, the business of Texas Petroleum and Refining, not secretive letters. Stevie should not have disturbed Mr. McElroy's business."

"Stevie did not intend—."

"Again, Millie, I am the wrong person. Stevie must speak with Mr. McElroy. He can probably find him at the doctor's office."

"At the doctor's? He said an explosion had happened. Is Mr. McElroy hurt?"

"No one was hurt, luckily. Send Stevie to Mr. McElroy."

"Is the drilling equipment destroyed?"

How much should I explain? Does Millie know the reason her brother was snooping? "I know very little about the oil patch," Nedda temporized. "Tab is at the grocer's, getting carpentry tools. You can ask him. Or will you continue to pretend to ignore Mr. Tabbert?"

The young woman's dark eyes widened. Horror aged her face. "He *told* you?"

Nedda needed a harder heart. "I guessed."

Millie sank against the door frame. "No one knows. He swore no one would know." Her palm planted on her belly.

That sign meant the same thing across many cultures. "Does he know?"

The question awoke a fire. She straightened with renewed energy. "He does not deserve to know!"

"Does Stevie know?"

The fire quenched. "No one knows."

"You must tell your mother. You must tell the doctor. And you must tell him."

"I do not want him if he does not want me."

"How do you know that he does not want you?"

"He is a man! He wants what is easy! A wife, a baby, we will not make his life easy."

"You do not know that unless you tell him."

Millie started to speak, then she whirled away and was gone. Her steps down the hall and the stairs were rapid, muting.

Well, that is an unexpected angle.

Nedda looked around Hank's room, at Colfax's cot with his pajamas folded neatly.

The world had suddenly changed.

She still didn't know the reason Stevie had snooped into Hank's documents, but she knew a scandal brewed.

Who else had guessed Millie's predicament?

. ~ . ~ . ~ .

Nedda stepped onto the planked porch of Milton's Grocery. The shade felt twenty degrees cooler than the blazing sunlit street. With a handkerchief borrowed from Hank, she dabbed at the sweat that had broken onto her upper brow and her neck.

Before she reached the door, it opened inward, the shop bell tinkling. Mr. Collier emerged, his green railroad visor still on his balding head. He clutched a paper-wrapped parcel tightly to his chest. Nodding at her, he left the door open and stepped off the porch, striding across the street to the saloon.

The air in the shop was stuffy with the day's building heat. Frank Milton glanced up as the bell rang again when Nedda shut the door. "Good day," she offered.

He muttered and hurriedly shut the cash drawer of the register. He stuffed his hand into his pocket.

"Do you have—?"

"I'll get Vera," he interrupted. He hastened to the door in the corner and went through, calling for his sister.

Nedda sighed and waited.

Vera Milton appeared, tying on her green shop apron. Her finely drawn features held little resemblance to her blockish brother. Golden curls haloed her face, brightening her blue eyes, a cornflower that reminded Nedda of her friend Isabella. Where Frank Milton was florid, Vera was tanned to honey. She and her younger brother Jeffrey topped her stocky brother by several inches. A trim figure completed her attraction.

The roustabouts had said only that the Milton's girl is "hands off" when Nedda had asked about her.

"How may I assist you, Miss Courtland?"

"I am in search of a hat that meets Mr. McElroy's standards. Wide-brimmed. And I dropped my powder puff this morning. I hope you have a replacement."

"Do you want a proper puff or one that fits into a compact?" Vera came around the counter and headed for a cabinet near the back. "Our stock is a little old, but if you do not want face powder, that should be fine."

"A proper puff."

She opened a drawer to display the stock. "Here's a pink one. Will that do?"

"Yes, of course."

On her return to the counter, she picked up a wide-brimmed hat with a low crown. Nedda nodded approval.

Vera bent over the store ledger to record the purchases. "Will this be all you need?"

"Yes When Hank—Mr. McElroy—described your town as the back of beyond, I brought two of everything I would need—except for the puff. Nor did I think I would need a hat."

"You wore a lovely cloche when you arrived that first day."

"Oh, thank you. Unfortunately, it does not shield me from your sunshine."

"It is the small things that we don't expect that always slip our minds." She named a sum as she punched the numbers on the register. The machine rang as she pulled the handle that opened the cash drawer.

Nedda handed over a twenty. "I do apologize. I have no change."

"This should be—." She stopped and frowned at the cash drawer. She lifted the tray to look under it. Her mouth thinned, and her eyes narrowed. Slowly she lowered the tray. "I do not have change for that. I will have it later, I promise. I will write what you owe in the ledger. Next time you come in, you can pay. Or I can write down how much change we owe you?"

"Why don't we do that? I'll pay the $20 on account, and you subtract what I bought. I am certain that I will have another purchase before we leave." Frank Milton's hasty behavior with the cash register was now obvious. Nedda had wondered how he had ready cash for poker at the saloon, for he lost nightly.

Vera tucked the $20 into her apron pocket and flipped open the ledger. "Nedda Courtland, correct? Address, the Donovan Hotel. How much longer will you and Mr. McElroy and the boy stay? Another week?"

"That I do not know. Mr. McElroy will decide."

"Is he a big name in Texas P & R?" She spun the ledger and indicated where Nedda should sign as she handed over the ink pen.

Nedda scanned the names above hers. Mr. Collier had a running total. Louisa Donovan, beans, rice, flour, salt, all for her café. Samuel Witt, cigars. Mrs. Turner, a bolt of cloth. She signed, adding a flourish at the end. "I am not certain what Mr. McElroy's position is. You know, we have never actually talked about that."

"Will he be the one who decides to stop the drilling?"

After this morning's explosion, the question seemed ominous. "I do not know that either." She laid down the pen and turned the ledger back.

"You don't know." Doubt was writ long on Vera's expressive face.

"That seems wisest, not to know," Nedda explained. "His business is not my business, although our businesses do align, somewhat."

The door bell tinkled, and both women looked. The mechanic Levi Green shut the door gently, stirring the merry bell again. His coveralls were wet with sweat and stained with oil and dirt.

Vera reached for a pack of cigarettes on a shelf behind her. "You look like you've had a hard morning, Levi."

"Wrestling with that old motor of Jose's. Ma'am." He acknowledged Nedda with a tap to his temple. "He thinks it will fetch a few dollars if it's working."

"And is it working?"

"It is. These cigs are my reward."

She slid the pack of Lucky Strikes across the counter. "These will rot your lungs, Levi."

"Maybe." He grinned, teeth bright in his tanned face. "One a day can't hurt me."

"One a day will stop a girl from wanting to kiss you."

Levi paused before he let the pack drop into the chest pocket of his coveralls. "I'll stop when I get me a girl. Know anyone looking for a man?"

Vera fluttered her pale lashes. "Why, Mr. Green, do you want a date with little ol' me?"

He guffawed. "Let's try tomorrow. Ma'am."

When the door shut and the bell stopped its tinkling, Nedda gave a wide-eyed look to Vera. "That sounded promising."

"If only." She flipped open the ledger, turned back a few pages, and made a quick note. "He'd be shocked down to his boots if I showed up at his door, expecting a date."

Nedda returned to the hotel, sweat prickling on her back, her good humor dashed.

Vera Milton deserved a good man and a life not as restricted as this no-name town. She was tied to her parents' store, the only child intent on making it prosper. Frank robbed it, and the youngest son Jeffrey had inhaled lung-damaging gas in the war, leaving him unable to do any strenuous work. The Miltons' livelihood depended on their daughter. Her shoulders looked too fragile to bear the burden.

Nedda had stayed too long in this town. Little tragedies crowded life here. Her travels with Mr. Ingram had kept her from colliding with most of the sorrows that shadowed people. But for a place with less than forty residents, Hartman County seemed to have a greater share of shadows.

Nedda passed Mr. Collier again as she reached the saloon. He left, lacking his parcel.

Stevie and his friend Manny, another mechanic at Ignacio's, snickered from their post on the bench beside the swinging doors.

"Oi, Mr. Collier, did my sister like your gift?"

Mr. Collier paused. He visibly squared his shoulders, then without looking around, he walked on. The youths dissolved into snorts and giggles, typical teenagers mocking adults.

Nedda scowled at them. They laughed harder.

She entered the shadowy saloon, nearly empty as the noon hour moved toward siesta.

"Ah, Miss Courtland, what a hat!" Behind the saloon bar, Mike Donovan polished glass pints. "A hat was what you needed. Will you have anything else that you need this afternoon? Will you help at the chapel again? The padre did ask."

"No, Mr. Donovan. Thank you, but I have paperwork that I must do." She glanced out the window where Stevie and Manny still laughed.

"Don't mind the boys, Miss Courtland." Levi Green sat near the stairs, a plate of rice and beans before him. "Might be good for Collier to hear he doesn't stand a chance with Millie. She's set her eyes on an oil man. None of us stand a chance until they leave."

"They do not need to mock him. He will be angrier."

"He starts as milquetoast. He'll have a long way to go before he's dangerous."

Nedda shook her head. She relived every moment of the explosion at the oil patch as she climbed the stairs. Anger that festered like acid often sought secretive means to damage and destroy.

None of us stand a chance until the oil men leave.

How many other men had their hopes for Millie crushed when the oil men arrived?

3 ~ Opportunity

On his return to their table, Hank detoured to glance at the chips stacked before the poker players. Grimness furrowed his brow and tightened his mouth and jaw.

Nedda placed a hand on the fold-over clutch in her lap, ready for trouble. She gave Hank a wide-eyed look. He shook his head.

He placed their beers on the table, sloshing foam, then handed Colfax a curvy green-glass bottle. "Slide over to my chair," he muttered to Nedda.

She didn't question him. He liked to face the door, but her seat gave a better view of the gamblers.

Colfax sipped his drink. "What is this?"

"Cola."

"Coca-Cola?" He named the brand overtaking most of the bottlers in Texas. "Stings like a gin rickey."

"A gin rickey?" Nedda turned very green eyes on the teenager. "What is that, and how do you know about it?"

"Don't panic, Miss Courtland. I've not fallen into bad habits while at the Sacred Heart Academy. Pater ordered one in Honolulu and let me have a sip. You would call it a gin and soda."

"A G & T?"

"Not the same thing at all." He sounded like a connoisseur. Taking a longer drink of the cola, he nodded at her untouched beer. "How's your ale?"

"Foamy."

"Foam's good for beer." Hank set down his pint. "Do you not want it?"

A long curse interrupted her. A man flung down his cards. They scattered over the poker table, knocking over stacked chips. Mr. Collier shoved back from the table.

"Losing again," Hank murmured.

"What else is new?" Colfax whispered.

Tab reached out to pull in the pot.

In her three weeks here, Nedda had rarely seen the railroad man win. Fuller was the sharp with Levi Green running a close second in winnings. Tab won often enough to be a regular threat. The others rotated the wins of occasional games.

"I did see Mr. Collier win once," Nedda quietly rebutted. "That was a big pot."

"You think he breaks even?" Colfax asked Hank who lifted a shoulder while his eyes scanned the men around the table.

Levi Green had gathered up the cards that spilled onto the floor then returned to his ladderback chair, his back to them. He began shuffling while the grocer's oldest son Frank Milton called for more beer. Donovan shouted for his daughter then hastened to draw another pitcher. Witt scooted his chair back and drew a cigar from inside his vest. Fuller muttered, and Witt laughed, hyena-loud, then he levered up and strolled to the bar.

Six men remained around the table. Of the roustabouts, O'Hara and Denny never played, O'Hara by choice and Denny because they pushed him out whenever he squeezed in. Based on the chips stacked before them, Tab and Leroy held their own tonight.

Collier and Green had three little stacks with coins scattered among the chips. Milton had only a few chips; he would return tomorrow night with fresh bills. "Robbing his pater's till," Colfax guessed during Nedda's one conversation with him about the nightly gambling, then he added, "Green never lets him sink too deep." The sixth man was Manny, Stevie's friend who worked with Green at Ignacio's Stable and Garage.

Fuller didn't have Green's qualms about taking everything Milton had. Green had to live here, though, while Fuller would leave when the drilling was finished.

If ever the drilling finished.

Collier leaned forward, watching the cards flash from Green's hands.

Stevie slid into Witt's abandoned chair and scooted to the table as his sister sauntered in from the kitchen.

"That's trouble," Hank muttered the obvious.

"Trouble with a capital T," Colfax added unnecessarily.

And it was. Stevie was the age of Denny and Colfax, yet the roustabouts still let the Donovan youth into their poker games. They took his money as easily as anyone else's.

Without refilling the men's pints Millie plopped the pitcher down in front of Green. Foamy beer sloshed onto the table and spattered a few cards. She bumped the man's shoulder, but he didn't react, just kept dealing, ignoring her.

"Ouch." Hank took refuge behind his pint.

Mr. Green flicked out the last card and set down the deck.

Stevie ignored his sister and gathered up his cards, wiping them on his shirt.

Manny slapped her buttocks.

Her brother exploded out of his chair and headed for the taller man.

Leroy jumped up and into his way. "Now, Stevie, Manny don't mean nothing by that. Millie can take care of herself."

The young woman had rounded on the mechanic. She slapped the back of his head. Manny swore and rubbed his head. Then he smiled. She stomped her foot and flounced back to the kitchen.

And the poker game resumed.

A movement at the bar caught Nedda's attention. Witt leaned on his elbow, puffing cigar smoke as he spoke to Mike Donovan. The hotel owner nodded then called to his son. "Stevie, give me a hand here."

"Dad, I'm in the game!"

"The game ain't started. You ain't ante'd yet. Come on. I need you to carry up a keg."

The youth grumbled but rose. "My cards——."

"I'll play them," Witt said.

"That's torn it," Colfax muttered, using slang he had picked up at the Academy. "Stevie will be a grouch until tomorrow night."

"Unless he wins a later game. Witt won't stay in long." Hank slid back his empty pint and eyed Nedda's beer. "You're not going to drink that, are you?"

"You have it." She scooted her chair back. "I'm going up. Good night." Hank started to stand, but she pressed down his shoulder. "No. You stay. Keep an eye on things."

"I'll go," Colfax volunteered. "You can have the rest of my cola."

Hank gave a mock shudder. "No, thanks."

As Nedda prepared to retire, she remembered that she hadn't told Hank about Stevie's snooping or Millie's predicament. She'd told Colfax about the snooping. Telling Hank about both problems could wait until morning. Nedda was not even certain she should involve herself in Millie's life.

Someone should.

The Donovans' older son and their sole daughter waded into quicksand. They both saw the danger, but they plowed on.

An hour later she blew out her candle. No one else had climbed the stairs, the ones inside or the outside balcony steps across from her east-facing window. A breeze fluttered the heavy curtains, scooping out the stifling air to replace with the cooling desert air. Cigar smoke wafted up and into her room, drifting through the old mosquito netting. Nedda folded her hands and prayed she would have a clear guidance for her involvement by morning.

She never expected the pistol shot that split the silence of the small hours.

. ~ . ~ . ~ .

The sharp report echoed as Nedda swam up from the drowning dream.

The second gunshot jolted her upright.

Then came shouts.

While she groped for her torch, footsteps raced past her open front window. She grabbed the torch and flicked it on. The light beam swung wildly and caught the shooter as he passed her east window, pelting for the stairs that descended from the balcony to the alley between the saloon and the neighboring building.

The mosquito netting tangled her, then she was through it and running for the east window. She pointed the torch beam at the stairs but caught only a dark hat as the shooter ran down the steps.

Then more running steps came.

She swung the beam.

Denny slid to a stop, caught in the beam. He flung up a hand to protect his eyes. "Did ya see `im? Did ya?"

"No. Who is shot?"

"Tab! I got to catch `im."

"No! Tab needs the doctor." The boy jittered on his toes, but her sharp command had steadied him. She set down the torch, aiming the beam at the stairs. "You have to bring the doctor here. How badly is Tab hurt?"

"He was cursing. Told me to go after `im."

"Get the doctor, Denny."

He gave a gulp and a nod and ran for the stairs. She withdrew into her room to find her wrapper and slippers. Then she snatched up her woefully-lacking medical kit and headed for the hall.

Men crowded the hall, then they sorted into the roustabouts, milling about as Fuller lit an old-fashioned candle sconce on the wall.

Colfax limped into the hall, shirt unbuttoned and khakis unbelted, only one boot on. He hopped on his foot as he shoved on the other boot. "I'm going for the doctor."

Nedda had a moment's consternation, for all the men had responded more quickly than she had. She had been lucky to see the shooter, but she seemed to have slogged through time after that. They were up, all half-dressed "I sent Denny, but you can hurry him along. Where's Hank?"

"With Tab." He headed for the interior stairs.

She passed Fuller tinkering with the second sconce. He was barefoot, his trousers sagging, his back shining with sweat. She heard footsteps on the stairs; one of the Donovans was coming to investigate.

Leroy and O'Hara stood in the doorway to Tab's room, but they moved when Nedda cleared her throat.

Hank had one knee on the bed as he bent over Tab. He had managed his trousers, and the torchlight gleamed over his tanned back. He pressed a wadded cloth to the foreman's shoulder. Blood stained the cloth, quickly darkening more of it. "Stay down," he gritted to Tab. "We need to stop the bleeding."

"Here." She handed her torch to O'Hara. "Keep my light steady, please."

Hank looked around. "You don't need to see this, Nedda."

"I've seen worse." She didn't explain where. He'd served in the Army. Beyond his spare information and her reply that she'd volunteered in London hospitals, neither had talked of the Great War. "Let me see."

O'Hara directed the beam at the cloth Hank held to Tab's wound. He lifted the wadding. Tab swore.

"Shut up. A lady's present."

The bullet had raked a gouge through skin before it dug into his meaty shoulder. O'Hara whistled. "A few inches, and you wouldn't be swearing, Boss."

Tab grunted and writhed when Hank re-applied the wadding.

"Nedda, where's Colfax?"

"Gone to hurry along the doctor. The Donovans are coming."

"No, they ain't," O'Hara growled. "Leroy?"

"On it. And I'll get a bottle of whiskey."

"Or two," Nedda added, "unless the doctor has a better antiseptic. Boiling water, too."

"Three bottles," Tab groaned, and Hank agreed.

Before Nedda felt the necessity of digging into her med kit, Dr. Turner arrived, with Colfax on his heels. He examined the wound quickly then shook his silvered head. "The bullet has to come out. That's best done in my office with better light. Stop giving him whiskey. It only slows his faculties." He ordered Hank and Fuller to assist Tab down the stairs.

"The Rangers have to be notified," Hank started.

Doc Turner lifted his hands from washing in the enameled basin. The water tinted pink. He shook them off then reached for his bag. "You can telephone them from my office, Mr. McElroy."

"You want us to do anything, Mr. Mac?" O'Hara asked, scratching at his whiskers. Trying to maneuver Tab down the stairs without hurting him, Hank didn't hear. The pusher waited, but without an answer, he handed back Nedda's torch and headed for his room.

Leroy watched O'Hara's door shut then headed for the stairs. "I'll go with 'em. Ain't got nothing else to do."

Colfax ran a hand through his mussed hair, the sweat-stiffened blond sticking several directions. "We should head back to sleep, too."

Nedda knew that would be impossible for her. "While you were out for the doctor, did you see anyone roaming around?"

"Not a soul. It's late. Shouldn't be any reason for people to be out and about."

"Not even Mr. Witt?"

"Nope, not even him. He didn't come out to check on Tab, did he?" He stared at the closed door of Witt's room, across from the stairs, then he headed for it.

"Wait, Colfax."

"It's best to know, isn't it?" He knocked on the door then again, harder.

O'Hara opened his door. He stepped out, dragging down his shirt. "Now that's curious."

"Did you see Mr. Witt?"

His bushy eyebrows raised, then he retreated. His door shut firmly.

Colfax knocked again then tried the doorknob. "Locked."

Nedda disappeared into her room then reappeared with her room key and a bobby pin. Her key fit. With a bit of wiggling, it turned the lock. The door swung open to an empty room. Colfax flashed around her torch, confirming no one was present.

"Give me that key." He locked the door then tried it on the lock for Fuller and Leroy's room. The key also fit the room he shared with Hank. He snorted. "Anyone can unlock our doors. We might as well not worry with locking them."

"Only someone with a key can unlock them."

"They leave the keys hanging on the board behind the hotel desk. Anyone can walk in, lift a key, and have access to everything. Prowl through all of our luggage."

"They wouldn't have much of a reason."

Colfax scowled at the floor then spoke softly. "Didn't you say Stevie looked through those mineral leases that Hank has?"

Nedda glanced along the hall. All remained quiet. Intercepted by Leroy, none of the Donovans had come upstairs. Closeted in his room, O'Hara wouldn't hear a hushed whisper. Nor would anyone lurking on the balcony. "The leases wouldn't do anyone any good."

"Unless they destroyed the lease."

"Hank only has a copy. The original remains at the Texas P & R office." The teenager's idea bloomed in Nedda's mind then struck a thorn. "Why would they want to steal or destroy a lease?"

"Delay the drilling. Force the company to drill elsewhere or give up entirely. Denny said they've been here close to a thousand days."

"And that's the reason for this morning's explosion?" The puzzle pieces slotted together. "Force the drillers to go elsewhere."

"That's it. TPR abandons the Buzzard, then someone swoops in and rakes in the profit."

"And they keep waiting, because Tab's turned stubborn about moving on."

"Denny says they've hit a lot of snags since Christmas."

"Half a year."

"That's either bad luck or a concerted effort to end the drilling."

"But why shoot Tab?"

"You said it, Nedda. Tab's turned stubborn about moving on."

"The crew can work without a foreman. They did for the first year and a half. They don't really need him, do they?"

"They need him to decide to abandon the lease."

"Or for Hank to decide."

"Yep. How patient is Hank? You know him best. Will he wait around, or will he push the drilling forward?"

She pointed out the obvious barrier. "No drilling until the new pipes arrive."

"And how long does he continue to drill?" His voice lowered to a hiss. "They could target Hank next."

They, they, they. Unknown and unseen conspirators who schemed for their own riches. Conspiracies with enemies everywhere. Convoluted and mysterious, the sphere for spies—the business that had Colfax's father in the Pacific Northwest, working on something for his fellow spy Emerson Werthy.

Nedda shook her head. "The simplest reason is usually the answer. Leave the drilling off to the side. Why would anyone target Tab?" Millie's predicament rang its sonorous bell.

Colfax gave an unexpected answer. "He raked in the final pot at the end of tonight. Hank told me."

"Really?"

"Really. And I missed it. Tab caught Manny cheating, and Levi Green threatened to tell his grandfather Ignacio. Leroy cashed out early because Witt kept standing behind him. Then that Mr. Collier claimed Milton was fudging the cards when he dealt. Didn't help him none. He still left with only his shirt. Mr. Collier argued with Tab about ignoring Millie, said he should thank her when she put the beer in front of him. Green told him to stop, but he kept picking at Tab. And they all thought Stevie had the winning hand. He had two pair, kings high, but Tab had a straight flush, all hearts. When he said he always won with the hearts, Hank thought Stevie or Collier would punch him, but neither did. Tab raked in over $300 at the end of the night."

"Really?"

He grinned at her, then a yawn split his young face. "I have to sleep."

"And I'm keeping you awake." She held out her hand. He looked at it blankly. "My key."

"No one needs a key," he reminded her.

"I want a little warning before someone invades my room."

"They'll come through your open windows. Unless you shut them. Then you'll swelter."

That comment sprang another idea. "How did the shooter target Tab? Did he shoot through the window? Or did he open the door then climb out the room window after he fired the pistol?" Colfax looked goggle-eyed. "Go to sleep," she relented. "You need it."

Once more in her room, she aimed her torch at her wristwatch. Close to 5. Sunrise would be around 7 o'clock.

She shed her wrapper and climbed on her bed to sit cross-legged, watching the wind shift the moonlight on the mosquito netting.

Fuller and Leroy returned a half-hour later, using the balcony stairs and climbing through the hall window, proving Colfax's point.

The first question, the greater one: Who had intended to kill Tab?

Who would risk murder to stop the drilling? That seemed extreme. Yet an accountant in New Orleans had committed two murders to hide his embezzlement.

The drilling would be profit for Texas P & R and whoever owned the land. Hank would know who owned the oil patch.

Who would profit if the drilling operation moved? Texas P & R had wasted nearly three years here. Wait, she did know who owned the neighboring property. Collier did.

Tab might advise the company to pull out entirely rather than pursue a new well.

If Collier knew about Millie's affaire, he would have an extra incentive to hate Tab. And the railroad man had lost money in tonight's game.

Who else had lost money? Stevie, who would also bear a grudge if he knew about Millie's baby.

Manny, who Millie ignored.

The way she ignored Tab.

Had something developed between Millie and Manny?

Frank Milton owned Tab money. And Fuller and Green.

Was money enough of a motive to murder?

Yes.

4 ~ Suspects

Dawn had greyed the sky when she heard steady steps climb the balcony stair.

Nedda slipped off the bed. Tying her wrapper, she bent to peek through the curtains. When she recognized the lanky figure, she stuck her head through the open window. "Hank?"

He came to her. "Did you sleep at all?"

She ignored the question. Worry hadn't let her shut her eyes. "How is Tab?"

"Doc Turner seemed pleased. He's keeping Tab there to tackle any infection."

"Did Tab say anything?"

"He didn't see who shot him."

"No, I wouldn't have expected him to, but anything else?"

"Not before the doc put him out. I rang the Texas Rangers." At her questioning eyebrows, he explained, "The Rangers are what passes for law in this county." He waited, but when she remained silent, thinking, he turned for the hall window.

"Denny didn't come back, not even when Leroy and Fuller did."

"Did he not?"

"You're not concerned?"

"Nedda, I don't think he shot Tab."

"Nor do I, but——. Look, climb in. I'll light a candle."

Her room had only one chair. After the candle created a warm halo, she flung back the mosquito netting and perched on the lumpy mattress.

He straightened from retrieving his wallet from the floor, slipping it into his back pocket.

"Button," she recalled.

"Not needed. Crawling through windows isn't going to be a habit."

She patted the place beside her.

He rubbed his nape. "Why are you worried about Denny?"

"I don't know. I just—did you know Witt wasn't in his room when Tab was shot?"

"Witt gone? Now that is odd."

"Would he have someone in town that he's involved with?"

"Don't know. Paloma's got twenty years or more on him." He named the hotel cook, the only unmarried woman of age in the town.

"Would he be involved with someone younger?"

He perched beside her as he considered it. "I think Donovan or

Ignacio would know if their wives weren't in their beds."

"The doctor's wife?"

"Nope. She worked with him tonight, handing tools and sponges and bandages."

"Mrs. Milton?"

"Too proper."

"Vera Milton?"

"Who? Oh, the grocer's girl. Witt wouldn't make a run for her, same reason as her mother. Who else?"

Nedda gave him a very green look.

He winced. "Millie? Is she that desperate to get her an oil man? Witt's three times her age. More."

"Who else would have his attention?"

"Um, I don't like to speculate without proof, but—." He stopped and held up a finger for silence.

Nedda strained to hear. Then a stair creaked.

Hank sprang up. He slipped to the window and bent down. Then, "About time you returned, Witt."

A surprised grunt, then heavy bootsteps crossed toward the window. "I don't remember that this is your room."

"It's Miss Courtland's room, as you well know. She and I are comparing notes."

He snorted. "Comparing notes is what you call it now?"

Nedda came beside Hank, clutching the tie on her wrapper. She thrust aside the curtain and pinned it to the wall with her hand. She had no reason to hide in the dark. They were talking about Tab's attempted murder, not involved in a salacious tryst as Witt implied. "We're wondering why Tab was shot."

Witt blinked. "What?"

The question didn't have the right tone. "Yes. As you know."

"Now how would I know, pretty lady? I wasn't here."

"Just where were you?" Hank snapped.

"Now, Mac, that ain't none of your business."

"I'm making it my business because Tab was shot. And you weren't here."

"When was he shot? After that poker game when he took everything that Collier and Milton and Green and that Donovan boy had?"

"You left before the game ended. When Manny threw that punch at Green."

Witt didn't respond to that. "When was Tab shot?"

Would the man answer every question with another question? No wonder Tab's directions to Witt devolved into argument. Nedda sensed Hank's frustration, already heightened and now climbing to the stratosphere.

"More than two hours ago. How did you know he took that last pot?"

"Where's Tab now? Laid out in his room?"

"At the doc's. I said he was shot. You hoping he was dead?"

"No," the driller shot back. "I didn't shoot him."

"Then where were you?"

"I ain't answerin' that."

"Have you seen Denny?"

"Hell, the boy's missing, too? Tab shot and Denny missing? You think the boy did it? You think he saw who did it?"

"I don't know what to think. He went to fetch the doc. He didn't stay there. He didn't come back here. You know the boy. Where would he go?"

"Dunno, boss. That's the god-honest truth. I don't know where Denny is. I don't know who shot Tab. I've got my thoughts on that."

"And what are those?"

"Best wait for the light of day before I say them."

"Sun's coming up, Witt. Say them now."

Witt stared east. The dawn had brightened, the sky above distant hills gone blue bright, the sunlight rimming the crest of the distant hill, the reflected radiance glinting on Witt's white stubble. "Don't know what to say, boss. Mebbe you should ask Fuller. Or O'Hara."

"Or maybe Colfax can tell us what y'all talked about while Tab and I were getting boards to rebuild the shack."

"He didn't hear nothing."

"Thank you for confirming my guess. Who will have the next job to sabotage our drilling?"

Witt's pouchy face shifted as he worked out Hank's claim, confusion arranging into dismay then gritty determination. His beady eyes shifted away then back. "You can't prove none of that."

"I don't need proof. I'll fire you, get the Rangers to haul you back to San Antonio, and hire new roustabouts."

"We didn't none of us shoot Tab. That's asking for trouble, boss. We'll have questions enough when a ranger gets here, and he won't take no guff off'n nobody. We wouldn't do that."

"Who all is we?"

"Me and Fuller."

"Leroy? Denny? O'Hara?"

"No. Reckon they knew, but they're not in on it. I swear, boss. Now that you know, we got no reason to continue messin' things up. We didn't shoot Tab."

"All right. I believe you. You'll stick around to answer the Ranger's questions, but I don't want either of you at the patch, never again. I'll have your money for you when the train comes in. Go on with you." And he turned his back on Witt.

Nedda let the curtain drop as Witt stomped to the hall window. The heavy curtain left them in the shadows as the day brightened. They heard creaks and rustlings as Witt climbed through the hall window. He didn't try to be quiet, and he scuffed his way to his room.

"What now, Hank?"

"Telephone Galvin." He named his boss at headquarters. "We've bigger problems than I thought. I reckoned they were fudging the depth of the hole. I didn't bargain on sabotage. It fits, though. Witt keeps Tab distracted. Fuller controls the engine. O'Hara strings the pipes. And refines the oil into diesel. He has to be involved."

"And Leroy?"

He shrugged.

"Denny?"

"He's a smart boy. Tab getting shot means all sorts of questions. If he's seen what they're doing and not doing, well—he gets a bad reputation on one oil patch, it carries throughout the whole industry. Witt and Fuller won't work in oil again. I'll telephone Galvin. The doc will still be up."

"You're going now."

"Yep. Going to see if I can get a new crew in with those pipes. Did you look over the license agreements?"

"I did. Stevie did as well."

"What? Stevie?"

"He had your attaché open and the papers spread out when I startled him."

Hank rubbed his face again. "I need coffee."

"Mrs. Turner will have a pot going, I'm certain."

He grasped her forearm. "You'll be safe here, you and Colfax. They know I know. They won't do anything to you—especially with Rangers on the way. The Rangers will be here before the train comes in, I guarantee."

"Do you believe Witt, when he says they had no reason to attack Tab?"

He gave that one-shoulder shrug then climbed out the window.

Nedda slipped onto the balcony as he ran down the wooden steps. She leaned on the balcony's stick railing as he crossed the street. Then she lingered, watching the day brighten, considering and re-considering all that Witt had said, all that she had wondered.

The saboteurs could have been desperate—but would they attack Tab when Hank could so easily order the drilling to continue?

Guilty of sabotage, then, but not attempted murder.

The drilling equipment would likely be missing a vital cog when the new pipes and crew arrived. That would prove where Witt had been. He might hold a grudge against Tab for something else, but he hadn't fired the pistol.

Nor had the others.

The shooter had to be someone local then. If they hated the drillers, they might target Tab, thinking that would stop everything. Or the shooter might owe Tab money.

And then there was Millie, centering a third motive.

What if Denny were the target, not Tab?

Nedda rejected that idea. Last night's desert moon had been a round silver. Everyone slept with open windows. Shining from the western sky, the bright moon lit the entirety of Tab and Denny's room whereas Nedda's room, on the eastern side of the hotel, missed out on that silvery illumination. The difference between Tab's big form on the four-poster and Denny's slight form on the cot would be obvious even in moonlight.

The shooter had pounded past her windows then scurried down the stair while she fought the mosquito netting. The only window with balcony access in Tab's room was on the hotel's front. She shivered. What had the culprit done while everyone slept, unaware of any danger?

She turned and looked along the balcony.

Something dark lay outside the front window of Tab's room.

Something dark like Hank's wallet, dropping out of his back pocket whenever he climbed through the window.

It *was* a wallet, the leather scuffed and worn with age.

Nedda picked it up then returned to her room. There, she turned it over and over before unsnapping it. Decent quality but old. And with no identification.

The wallet could not have been dropped yesterday before sundown. Millie's little brother Charlie had swept the balcony then, his last chore of the day.

Witt hadn't dropped it. The balcony didn't run on the hotel's west side. He accessed his room from the outside stairs on the east then either climbed through the hall window or walked around to his window on the south.

Not Witt's, then.

Whose? The shooter, for certain.

He would have half-climbed through the window to have the best aim at Tab.

Nedda shuddered and jerked shut her curtains, streetside then the east.

She prayed no one had seen her pick up the wallet.

But if it had already been missed by the culprit?

The shooter would be desperate to retrieve it.

She searched through several slots for papers—all empty, a ticket stub worn thin and faded green but no folded notes or bills. In the longer divided slot across the top, she found a few loose $1s then more, a wealth of money. A week's wage and more, two weeks, maybe three. And there, tucked behind a weathered photo, four folded $20s.

The photograph was of Millie, her head tilted back to highlight the glory of her wavy hair, the lovely angle of cheek and chin and neck, and the sultry smolder of half-lidded eyes. The photo had to be new, but it looked worn at the edges. The wallet's owner had handled the photo many, many times.

Who would receive this temptress' photo from Millie?

Manny Ignacio? Would he have a wallet like this? He could.

Frank Milton? Nedda rejected that—then placed the man back on her mental list. Millie might have viewed him as a potential escape before the drillers came to Hartman County.

Who else?

Levi Green? She couldn't see the mechanic mooning over Millie, but most people hid their secret desires. He could have a wallet like this, bought when he was still flush with cash from wartime pay.

Who else?

5 ~ Revelation

"Morning, Miss Courtland"

The boy stood at her window, peering around her room.

Nedda gave a last flick of her hairbrush. "Good morning, Charlie. I see you have your broom. I thought you swept the balcony last evening."

"I did, Miss, I did. I'm lookin' for somethin'."

She screwed on her earrings, the ones with the dangling green glass that matched her eyes, then picked up her fold-over clutch. "Looking for something? What have you lost?"

"I didn't lose it. It got misplaced. I said I'd look for it."

"What is lost, Charlie?"

"You didn't find anythin' on the balcony?"

"No, I didn't. What are you looking for?"

"Oh, nothin'."

"What is lost will be found," she said lightly while her heart raced. Had Millie ordered her little brother to look for the wallet? Or Stevie?

Had Millie or Stevie shot Tab?

Charlie had vanished. She peeked out the window. He didn't attempt to sweep as he walked along the front balcony.

Downstairs, she joined Colfax. He grunted at her but kept shoveling in the *huevos rancheros*. Two of the roustabouts sat at the window, drinking coffee. Mr. Donovan and his wife were absent.

"Good morning to you, too." She slid across from Colfax.

He stopped eating with a rueful grin. "Millie said she'd bring another plate when I finished this one."

"And why are you—how does Hank say it?—why are you in such an all-fired hurry this morning?"

"I'm going with Denny and them to the site. We still have the shack to build."

"Really? Who is in charge of this expedition?"

"Fuller and Leroy." He motioned to the men sitting beside the front window, talking quietly. "O'Hara's not going."

"And Witt?"

"I don't know about Witt."

"He might just roll over and sleep in, with Tab not there to crack the whip."

"I think Hank is a bad influence on your language, Nedda."

She smiled then remembered the sabotage Witt had revealed. "Does Hank know your plans?"

"I haven't seen him, not since we went to the doctor's."

"Colfax—." She changed her advice. "Take a second look before you leap."

He grinned, no longer the somber English youth released from his public school. "Unlike the pater, you mean? Look, Millie, I finished."

"I do see, Mr. Ingram. Do you wish eggs this morning, Miss Courtland?"

She scanned the young woman's expression. Millie wore a smiling mask. "Black coffee, please."

She withdrew the photo while Millie retrieved another cup and the coffee pot from the kitchen.

"I saw a photo of you," she said as Millie poured the coffee, black and strongly aromatic. "You looked a Hollywood starlet. Your hair was long and luxurious."

The coffee pot wavered. "I don't know about any photograph."

"Truly?" She placed it on the table, face up.

Colfax inhaled sharply then looked up at Millie. "Jeepers, that's a photo! You look gorgeous, Millie. I'd like one."

The young woman lifted her gaze from the photograph and met Nedda's. "How long have you had this?"

"I found it this morning. It's a lovely photo. Do you have any more?"

She set the wavering coffee pot beside Colfax's plate. "No, I do not have more. Just two. I kept one and gave another to Tab."

"Are you certain you did not receive three? To whom did you give that one?"

Millie flinched.

"Mr. Collier?"

"That man! No!" But her gaze cast away, to the listening roustabouts.

"Manny?"

She laughed. "He's a bad one. I do not want to encourage him."

"He is indeed a bad one. Who received the third photograph?" Nedda knew who she wanted the recipient to be.

"We owe him, him and his father, since before the oil men came. I did not want—."

"Frank Milton?" Never would she have guessed him.

Millie's eyes fluttered shut. She nodded. "Give it to me," she whispered.

"I'll keep it."

She whirled away and fled to the kitchen.

Colfax whistled. "Frank Milton and Millie? No way. Here, where did you find that photo?"

"A wallet fell on the balcony last night. I found it this morning." The two roustabouts stared at her. "Stuffed with cash," she added. In that moment she knew Millie had lied. Frank Milton had blown all of his money in the poker game. He wouldn't have kept a reserve. He wasn't the culprit.

"Last night on the balcony? Hey, you think Milton shot Tab?"

"I do not. It doesn't ring true."

"No? Then who?"

Charlie rushed into the saloon from the kitchen. He hung over a chair, scowling at Nedda.

Stevie came more slowly, swaggering, hands in the pockets of his baggy dungarees. "Good morning, Miss Courtland." Millie appeared in the kitchen door, with the cook Paloma peering around her.

Nedda slipped her hand inside her clutch, seeking the Webley her former employer had gifted her. "Good morning, Stevie."

"I think you found something that does not belong to you, Miss."

"What did I find? To whom does this photograph belong? Not to you, I think. No, definitely not you."

"That's a foolish game you're playing, Miss."

"Nedda," Colfax whispered in warning.

"I am not playing a game. Whoever dropped this thing I found, that person shot Mr. Tabbert. He is at the doctor's, recovering."

"He will live. We all heard this."

"He is lucky. Two inches, and he would be dead. Killed. Murdered."

"But he's not dead. It's not a crime then."

"Here now," Leroy protested.

Nedda kept her eyes on Stevie, watching his hands, watching the shift of his body. "Murder was attempted," she countered. "That's a crime. The Texas Ranger will agree with me."

"You need to give me what was found."

"And how will that help, Stevie? We all know. Colfax and I, Fuller and Leroy. Paloma. The whole town will know. Do not add to the problem. Do not get involved in this."

He shook his head then drew his hands out of his pockets. One held a short-barreled revolver. He pointed it at her. But his hand shook. He wasn't the shooter. "Give it to me."

"I don't have it," she lied. "I gave it to Mr. McElroy this morning. I kept out this photo to question Millie."

"You don't have the wallet?"

"No, I do not. You will have to tell Mr. Collier that it is impossible to get."

"He won't like that."

"No, I suppose he will not."

Colfax shot into movement, slinging the coffee pot at Stevie.

The gun exploded as the pot destroyed the youth's aim. The bullet shattered glass.

Then Colfax leaped upon Stevie and tackled him to the ground. Fuller and Leroy jumped into the fight.

Charlie came in with his broom until Nedda fired the Webley. The bullet imbedded in a weathered board at the boy's feet.

Colfax released Stevie. Dusting himself off, he retrieved the pistol, fallen to the floor and dripping with black coffee and grounds. "Sit. All of you," he ordered, nodding at Millie.

Minutes later, Hank and Mr. Milton burst into a silent tableaux, Stevie and Charlie were watched over by Leroy and Fuller. Millie cried softly as she rocked in a chair. Nedda and Colfax stood behind the bar, watching both entrances to the room. They lowered their pistols as the men glared, breaths heaving from their run from the store to the saloon.

"You'll want to visit the depot," Nedda advised. "Mr. Collier dropped his wallet on the balcony last night when he tried to kill Tab."

"Collier?" Hank asked as Millie burst into a wail. He winced.

"Colfax, give him the weapon."

The youth handed it over. "A Police Positive. 32 gauge. That's the bullet that the doctor pulled out of Tab, isn't it?"

Hank examined the Colt 32. "This explains why Tab's not dead, just wounded."

"Lucky," Nedda repeated the word she'd said to Stevie. "And Mr. Collier is trying to involve these three to deflect suspicion from himself. He'll have to pay for that. He may have bribed them."

"Did he give you money?" her tall Texan demanded.

Stevie nodded slowly. "Enough to leave here."

Oh, the hope of a new life elsewhere. How often did that drive people into foolish actions? Nedda remembered the money in Collier's wallet, still in her clutch. "He didn't have enough money for that."

"With what Tab won—."

Hank shook his head. "Not enough, not for all three of you. Or was he going to let you brothers go and keep Millie here with him?"

The young woman's sobs had slowed as her brother revealed the plan, but at Hank's question she broke into louder wails. To stay here, when she had dreamed of escape, even more than her brothers had—.

Collier had another pistol, an old revolver from the Civil War. When Hank and Mr. Milton neared the depot, he shot at them. The service pistol exploded in his hand.

When the Texas Ranger arrived at sunset, Doctor Turner was still trying to save his hand.

.~.~.~.

One thousand one hundred and eleven days after the drilling started, Tab argued with the new driller. Another pipe was strung then lowered into the hole chipped out by the drill.

It started as a rumble, distant thunder as the Texas sun blazed on the oil patch.

The pipes shuddered and skirled in the hole. Then the well blew, black oil spewing higher than the derrick, soaking Leroy high in the air, dousing the new motorman and O'Hara and Denny, spattering Tab and the new driller. The men whooped. They slapped each other's backs. Denny danced a jig while Leroy yodeled from the top of the derrick.

Nedda scrubbed at the oil spattered on Hank's cheek.

"Never mind that," he said and caught her around the waist, drawing her close. "I'm not a man for traveling the world, Nedda Courtland. I don't think you'll get me to London anytime soon. I'll never be anything but a roustabout that got lucky when I found you. But I've a ring in my pocket that's wanting on your finger."

"Were you waiting for the oil to come in before you asked me?"

"Yes and no. You're running Ingram & Son Investments. You're a woman with independent means. You don't need me, Nedda. Makes a man wary."

"No, Hank, I don't need you. I *want* you."

He grinned, blue eyes glinting above oil-spattered cheeks. "Will you marry me? Soon?"

"Should I answer yes and no?"

His embrace tightened.

She flung an arm around his neck, not caring about the oil still raining upon them. "Yes, Hank. Yes and yes!"

. ~ . ~ . ~ . ~ . ~.

GULF
Storm

COURTING TROUBLE BOOK 3

M. A. LEE

Gulf Storm

1 ~ Bribe

Nedda dangled her legs off the sun-silvered dock. Her toes grazing the water, she exchanged glances with the alligator floating yards away, its yellow eyes and armored crown skimming the surface.

She sat in tree-cast shade, on the edge of the blazing sunshine. Two bands of greyish clouds filled the southeast horizon. Birds barely sang through the heat. A heron crept forward on her right, the bank of the bay marshy there and filled with stiff cattails.

She didn't look away from the `gator. Fresh in memory was its supper last evening, an unwary spoonbill. The frantic flapping wings before the alligator submerged to drown its victim still gave her chills.

A sweet soprano drifted over the bay waters. She leaned forward and spotted the canoe on the inland edge of Back Bay. Mr. Culpepper rowed while his wife in her wide-brimmed straw hat sang "Alice Blue Gown" to the silent birds. Nedda smiled, for her bridal gown looked like some depictions of that. Tomorrow evening she would wear the champagne gold frock. Pearl beads adorned the gossamer lace attached to the chemise bodice. Beneath a silk banded waist, the gossamer lace repeated in decorative scoops over the gathered skirt. The sheer lace and light silk were perfect this late summer season.

Bare feet struck the dock, coming toward her. The alligator sank. She lifted her legs onto the hot dock, the heat quickly drying her skin.

A lanky figure in a white shirt and baggy cut-off khakis dropped beside her. "You've missed another argument," Colfax said.

Draping the pleated skirt of her tennis dress, Nedda wrapped her arms around her knees and scanned the youth. He'd changed over the summer, less skinny boy and more wiry young man. The sun had kissed his blond hair to flax and tanned his pale English skin. The weeks in west Texas had changed him mentally as well. Attempted murder of someone in a close circle had sobered his childish bents. His grandfather's death in the late spring hadn't really registered with Colfax until Rhode Tabbert was shot. His enthusiasm for pranks had vanished then.

She leaned her head on her knees, blocking the sun from directly entering her eyes. "Another argument?"

"You missed the one at breakfast?"

"I returned upstairs," she reminded him. "I had to change. I didn't think we would play tennis this morning."

"Too hot for this afternoon." He glanced at the Culpeppers. "Too hot for boating. This shade's nice." He stretched out beside her. "It's as hot as it was in Oman."

"Who was arguing this morning?"

"Same as who's arguing now. Hank and Ray."

"Two arguments in the same day?"

"Yep. And one yesterday. Makes me wonder if they're truly friends."

She eased out a breath, hunting a diplomatic way to relate her fiancé's assessment of his old friend. "Hank did say Ray could be difficult."

Colfax snorted. "Did Hank forget what difficult truly means?"

He had wisdom beyond his peers. Had traveling the world granted that discernment? Or had he aged in his scant two months at the Sacred Heart Academy? He was a stranger there, his classmates and masters completely unknown to him, the culture of a Catholic boarding school in northern Louisiana alien to an English prep-school boy.

A splashing caught her attention.

Mr. Culpepper was rowing out into the bay, avoiding the marshy bank to avoid tangling in the cordgrass and saltgrass and duckweed. Mrs. Culpepper leaned over the canoe, peering into the water.

This weekend would be a moneymaker for the Bells, owners and hosts of the Back Bay Inn. Nedda, Hank, and Colfax had arrived late Thursday afternoon. Waiting on the porch, watching them unload suitcases, was Ray Anderson, Hank's best man. The men had attended university together. Their friendship deepened in war. Yet her whiskers twitched as she shook his hand, limp ice. His yellowed eyes and the heavy bags that sagged onto his sallow cheeks betrayed dissipation.

Ray sidestepped Hank's question about his early arrival at the inn. In west Texas, a saboteur had avoided answers by asking more questions. Nedda learned from her late employer never to trust a man who wouldn't answer a direct question.

Ray had then introduced them to his date for the wedding, one Pearl Lawrence, a brassy blonde whose scooped blouse and tight skirt displayed her assets. Hank had taken a deep hissing breath, but he held his tongue. "I work in Galveston," Pearl announced then introduced them to her employer at the dance club, one Al Rogers, natty in a slim-fitting pin-striped suit with narrow lapels. Rogers offered a jolly smile that didn't crinkle his eyes. A diamond flashed on his finger as he shook their hands.

Watching from the corner was the quiet giant "Mr. Jerry Phillips. He drove us. He was a boxer," Pearl added, a bit of pride in her voice.

Mr. Phillips' broken face testified to his years in the boxing ring. He wore a dark double-breasted suit that strained over his broad shoulders. He measured Hank and Colfax then dismissed Nedda with a single glance, not knowing her Webley weighted her fold-over clutch.

The first argument between Hank and Ray started at dinner. Ray claimed that Hank said he could bring a date; Hank declared that he'd never promised that. The petty dispute ended with the arrival of the dessert when both Mr. Rogers and Mr. Phillips vowed they didn't expect an invitation to the wedding. "We plan to fish, isn't that right, Phillips?"

"Yes, sir, Mr. Rogers."

Silent throughout the argument, the Culpeppers shared over coffee in the parlor that they were happenstance guests. "We booked our cottage in May. We never expected a wedding. I'm excited about it."

"Thank you. We hoped to have a small wedding," she shared with the couple. "Hank found this inn when he came to Chambers County for his work."

"You're English," Mrs. Culpepper gushed, and Nedda had to answer a multitude of questions about the royal family and the future monarch. Eventually, the woman asked the reason Nedda had chosen a wedding at the Back Bay Inn rather than in Houston.

"My only requirement for the wedding was tranquility. Hank promised that this was the perfect place. It is beautiful here by the bay, everything green and lush."

Now Mr. Culpepper allowed the bay's current to catch the canoe. It pivoted and skimmed toward the inland shore. His wife resumed her dreamy song, muted by a gust of wind.

Nedda returned to Colfax's talk of arguments before her thoughts had distracted her. "What started the second argument? I saw the bruise on Hank's cheek. I never expected fisticuffs."

"What? Oh, that." He stirred. The sun had cast over enough to burn his foot. Colfax levered up his leg and rubbed his reddened toes.

"You did bring up the arguments."

He grinned and returned to his supine position. "Something about Texas Petroleum and Refining. I didn't stay to listen."

"But Hank receives a bruise on his cheek."

"You should see Ray's black eye."

"I thought you left."

"I stayed for the fisticuffs."

"Is Ray with Texas P & R?"

"I don't think so."

The oil industry had more dry wells than gushers and mineral licenses that they let lapse, but the companies pumped vast amounts of cash into the pockets of its owners, investors, and workers. Nedda had worked with Hyatt Ingram, a global venture capitalist in petroleum, and she inherited enough shares in his company to stay abreast of the industry.

In her home of England, the status line divided blue-blooded nobility from red-blooded workers. In Texas, that line divided the booming oil industry from everyone else. Background didn't matter; oil did.

For its proximity to the famous Spindletop gusher, Houston had boomed, but the state's entire east coast had had a roaring economy for over two decades. West Texas had lagged behind the east, but the Buzzard No. 3 well in Hartman County promised to kindle a boom out there.

Was his old friend Ray pushing Hank about Texas P & R? Did he have any fingers in the petroleum pie. If not, he would backpedal into obscurity while his friends rolled in black gold. Those friends headed here, a groomsman for Hank named Paul Jackson, married to Hank's sister, and Boone Galvin, a war buddy who served as TP&R's president.

Had Hank considered any of that when he asked Ray to be his best man? No. He remembered the war, when they had each other's backs during battle, and he harked back to their college days, when their futures shone brightly.

One worked for the black gold. The other aimed for fool's gold.

That drove Ray's resentment.

"No doubt," she offered mildly, "we'll hear the reason for both arguments before dinner."

Colfax grunted. He threw an arm over his eyes. "Let me nap, Nedda. Haven't played tennis in months."

The sun peeked through a wide arc of clouds and glinted on the bay waters. A dragonfly buzzed over the youth. He didn't stir, and the flyer passed over. A spoonbill flew past, white wings widespread as it soared above the waves, restless as the tide came in. Oaks on the distant shore created a lush green backdrop.

Nothing moved, the bay waters tranquil, a stronger breeze cooling the perspiration on her arm, all quiet and peaceful. The atmosphere she wanted for her wedding. After four years of global jaunts with her former employer Hyatt Ingram, this settled peace lured her.

Hank had known the perfect spot for their nuptials.

She closed her eyes and remembered the long drive here.

Only in the last few miles had the land drawn her. Piney woods enclosed the hard-packed dirt of the road to the back bay area. A planked bridge crossed a little silver creek that separated the island from the country propre. Their tires had rumbled across the bridge, sending birds into the air at the unusual thunder.

When the road swung away from the bay waters, the trees opened back to reveal the white-washed Back Bay Inn. Columns supported three stories of porches. A riotous garden bordered the front porch and framed wide steps. Nedda had sighed at the glory of star pentas, zinnias and salvia, backed with globe amaranth.

In the cooler shadows inside the inn, zinnias graced the check-in desk of the entryway while three bouquets decorated the long dining room table, open to the hallway. She discovered later that the host's wife Mrs. Bell freshened the flowers daily while her two daughters-in-law ran the maids and the kitchen.

Bootsteps hit the planks of the long dock. She lifted her head and gave a smile to the younger of the Bell sons. "Hello, Eddie."

Colfax stirred, proof that he hadn't been asleep. He sat. "Going fishing in the twilight?"

Eddie grabbed the line for a dinghy bobbing alongside the dock and began towing it to shore. "Bringing the boats in. Storm's coming from the Gulf."

Wide bands of clouds swirled to the south, white and puffy in the outer bands, greying toward the southeast.

The wedding! "When is the storm expected?" Nedda rolled to her feet and brushed off her tennis dress.

"Landfall's tonight or early Saturday. The wee hours."

Landfall was an odd term to use for a storm.

"Will it be gone by Saturday evening?"

"Should be pushed through by then. Dad has better answers for you, Miss Courtland. I need to get these boats in." He dropped into the water's edge and began towing the red dinghy onto the bank.

"I'll give a hand," Colfax volunteered. "All these boats, Eddie?"

"All of them. Thanks for the help. We need to get them past the trees."

The youth measured the distance from the dock, a good 30 feet although the bay's bank was only six or so feet. "That's high."

"Might have a storm surge twice that. Grab this." He tossed a rope to Colfax then reached for the blue dinghy nudged in the cattails at the bank.

Nedda waited until they had wrestled the blue dinghy up the bank then started for the inn.

An engine's putter drew her attention to the road.

Bright yellow flashed through the piney woods then emerged. A new Cadillac Phaeton rolled slowly over the dirt so it didn't stir up dust. Two people sat in the front seat, and Nedda added a spurt to her step to meet them at the inn.

The Cadillac stopped before the steps as the inn door opened. The senior and junior versions of the Bells came onto the porch. The engine cut. A man slipped out and headed around the hood as Nedda reached hearing distance.

"Welcome to the Back Bay Inn," Mr. Bell said. "Junior, help them with their luggage."

The man opened the passenger door. A woman slid out. Her hat came into view, a cream-colored cloche with a dark ornament. She wore a cream dress covered with polka dots. The man offered his hand then led her up the steps while Junior opened the trunk, American for boot. He lifted out a valise and two suitcases.

Mr. Bell ushered the couple inside. "My wife will assign your room. What's that? Oh yes, they arrived late yesterday," and Nedda realized who this couple had to be. "Mr. and Mrs. Paul Jackson" was the name she'd written on the envelope, but Mrs. Jackson was Hank's sister Flo, and the man had to be his groomsman and work colleague Paul Jackson.

She bypassed the luggage and approached as the man bent to sign the desk ledger. "Florence Jackson?" she ventured, extending her hand. "I'm not quite certain where Hank is. I am Nedda Courtland."

The woman turned. Only then was Nedda certain, for she looked upon a feminine version of Hank: tall, slender rather than lanky, with those startling blue eyes and high cheekbones.

"Call me Flo." Her handshake was firm but gentle and quick. She had Hank's drawl, and humor sparkled in her blue eyes. "I'll have words with my brother later. He is an atrocious correspondent, and his telegrams are worse. He never mentioned that you are English. Or how you met. Or the reason he didn't bring you to visit. One telephone call from a god-forsaken place in west Texas, then in another call he's tells me that he's found his woman and *she* wants me to be her maid of honor."

"Hartman County in west Texas," Nedda supplied, "and it is god-forsaken. Less so now that oil's come in."

"Buzzard No. 3," her husband added, joining their conversation.

"You men do not know how to name oil wells. Miss Courtland, this is my husband Paul."

"Hello. Flo, I do regret that we had no time to visit. Until Monday we were in west Texas. Tuesday he spent at Texas P & R headquarters—."

"Yes, Paul saw him there. And that's all they did, see each other in passing." She gave a wry grimace.

Her husband's eyes twinkled. "He was in meetings with Galvin. I was meeting with our engineers."

"Men have no accounting of what is most important. My brother's fiancée is more important than test patches and drill samples! But Hank could have brought you to me on Wednesday."

Nedda shook her head. "That was not at all possible. You see, I needed a bridal gown."

"Oh, yes! What did you—?"

"Flo, honey, let's delay this a bit," her husband interrupted. "Once you start talking about the wedding, an hour will pass."

"Oh, Paul! But I am that interested. An hour on the wedding, an hour on your first meeting with my brother, a third hour on his proposal. Give me fifteen minutes to freshen up, Nedda."

"Would you like tea? Or lemonade? We can have it in the parlor." She glanced to Mrs. Bell for approval.

That woman was avidly listening. She tapped the desk bell four times. "Lemonade and cookies, yes?"

"Perfect, Mrs. Bell."

"Find that brother of mine," Flo urged. "I need to bend his ear about the proper treatment of his bride."

"Clarrie." Mrs. Bell handed a key to her oldest granddaughter. "Second floor, Room H."

As the Jacksons started behind Clarrie, Junior Bell came with a suitcase in one hand, a valise tucked under his arm, and a train case in his other hand.

Nedda leaned over the desk. "My key, please, Mrs. Bell. I should freshen up before tea with my future sister-in-law."

"Lemonade and cookies will be waiting in the parlor when you come down, Miss Courtland."

. ~ . ~ . ~ .

Although the windows were opened to admit the breeze, the plantation shutters were closed, shadowing the parlor. The slats were angled to diffuse the light. Remembering dreary summer days of her childhood, Nedda gloried in the Texas sunlight, brighter than London's had ever been.

The promised tray—with a pitcher, glasses, and a tray of cookies—rested on the coffee table before the lengthy Chesterfield sofa when Nedda reached the parlor, fresher through the swift use of soap, water, powder, and a slimming handkerchief frock with a diamond print.

She entered as the sleek-suited Al Rogers swiped cookies from the tray.

At her appearance he smiled. His eyes still didn't reflect anything. "Caught with the goods."

"Please, help yourself to some lemonade, too. I can ring for more glasses. Mr. Phillips," she knew he was there but she had to look over her shoulder to spot him in a dimmer corner, "do have some cookies. Do you want lemonade?" She rang the metal bell resting on the mantel. A crewel-worked bell pull hung to the mantel's left, but she doubted it still connected to the servants' call board. "Shall I bring you a plate of cookies?" She laded four onto a plate as she asked.

"No, ma'am. Miss. None for me, Miss."

"A shame. These are lemon, too, I think. Quite refreshing in this heat, don't you think so, Mr. Rogers?"

He dusted cookie crumbs from his fingers with an embroidered handkerchief. "Quite refreshing," he echoed, mimicking her accent.

Nedda gave him a sharp look.

Mrs. Bell appeared. "These gentlemen would like lemonade and cookies as well, Mrs. Bell. Is that possible?"

While she shot a glance at Mr. Rogers, the older woman avoided looking at Mr. Phillips' ruined face. "Of course, Miss Courtland." She retreated, and in seconds they heard the desk bell ring out several times.

"A ring for each grandchild?" she mused aloud

"That would account for it. Did I hear you right, Miss Courtland? Your wedding is Saturday?"

"Yes, that's correct. Rev. Thomas—he dined with us last evening—."

"Before Ray Anderson stuck his oar in."

"Um, yes? Rev. Thomas will perform the ceremony."

"And Anderson's still best man?"

"Yes." Nedda elongated the word, her whiskers twitching again. She glanced at Mr. Phillips, but he remained stolidly stoic.

"Know what you're in for, marrying an oil man?"

"I do not have on blinders, Mr. Rogers."

"You like horseracing?"

The question almost seemed a *non sequitur*, but a wary whisker warned that it was not. "Steeplechases."

"That's where they jump." He nodded. "Higher risk. Higher bets. Your bet must be pretty high on your man. He's got secrets, though. My friend Anderson knows what they are. It's dangerous when somebody knows your secrets. Even more dangerous when those secrets get shared with a loose-mouthed girl like Pearlie."

Voices stopped him, then Flo entered the parlor, talking over her shoulder to her husband.

And Hank.

Hank was here, scowling when he caught sight of Al Rogers and Jerry Phillips.

Does he know these two men from Galveston, or is he merely displeased at their presence in the parlor?

Nedda hated herself for wondering. Tomorrow she would marry Hank. Critiquing his acquaintances before she'd had more than a couple of hours in their presence seemed disloyal.

Mr. Rogers stood, buttoning the slim-fitting jacket with its bold pinstripe. "Good day to you, Miss Courtland." He walked out. Jerry Phillips followed.

Flo cast herself onto the sofa. "Tell me everything! How you met my brother. When you met him. How he won your heart. How he proposed. When he proposed. When you decided on this weekend for your wedding. How you planned a wedding from all the way over in west Texas! And how you bought a bridal gown in one day. One day! I took weeks to decide on my gown. I want to know everything!"

Her husband groaned. "Beware, Miss Courtland. My wife will ask questions until she has all the answers." He palmed several cookies. "Where's your roadster, Hank? I didn't see it."

"Needed more space. I'm in the Packard Touring Car."

"The green one? Nice. Come see my new Phaeton."

Hank swiped a handful of cookies and left with Paul Jackson.

"How you met my brother," Flo prompted. "When and where and

how and why."

Nedda launched into the story that began in New Orleans with poison and death.

She didn't remember her conversation with Al Rogers until much later.

2 ~ Conspire

An early afternoon rainstorm killed the day's heat, yet a later storm left the air muggy, a sticky humidity that offered little relief.

Next to arrive was Mr. Stringer who brought news of an approaching hurricane. He complained that the wind had pushed his Oakland coupe toward the ditches as he drove from Houston to the coast and the Back Bay area.

Mrs. Bell switched on the large radio behind the hotel desk. The broadcast predicted an overnight landfall south of Galveston before it resumed jazz offerings. The music during preparations for dinner.

As they gathered before dinner, Pearl Lawrence brought up Galveston and the sea wall, asking how the hurricane would affect Back Bay. "We flooded" was all Mrs. Bell said.

"Lost over ten oaks," Mr. Bell added. A cracking branch stressed his words.

Mr. Stringer quickly turned the conversation with a description of a wild evening in the town. He continued with more shenanigans at clubs and speakeasies and coastal cottages.

The rain started, a heavy downpour that abrupted stopped. Only a few minutes passed before it resumed. This time it didn't stop.

When the wind rattled the double-hung windows, Mr. Bell stood. "Already?" his wife asked.

"Ring for the boys." He left, and they soon saw him outside a dining room window, unfolding the plantation shutters. The wind hissed as it blew through the slats. Then he snapped the slats shut and locked a bar over the shutters, preventing the slats from moving. Junior Bell appeared to close the other dining room shutters, and the guests heard the bar across another shutter lock into place.

The wind became a steady force streaming around the house.

Then Eddie came in. "Water's all choppy. The bay's flooding over the dock. I need to pull the boats further up. Anybody give me some help?"

"I will," Colfax said quickly, and the TP&R men agreed. Ray shook his head when Hank asked "Coming?" He glanced at Al Rogers who continued eating his apple cobbler.

The men headed upstairs to fetch their slickers and galoshes.

The women rushed to the front porch to watch. On the straw mat was a colorful painted bunting, plumage bright and neck broken. Flo knelt to gather it into her cupped hands. She slipped out of her shoes then pattered barefoot across the grey-painted boards. She dropped the bird over the railing, into the rain-beaten flowers, then came back, shaking the water from her hands. Her legs and feet were soaked.

They stayed against the wall, for the wind-driven rain washed the front of the porch. The day had darkened into an early twilight. The steady gusts bent the trees inland. Beyond them was the haze of trees near the shore. The pelting rain couldn't obscure the billowing bay, whitecaps breaking over the dock.

Lights flashed, heralding a low-slung vehicle traversing through the piney wood. More lights shone behind the dark touring auto. It slid as it negotiated the road's turn toward the inn. The rear fishtailed, but the driver steered into the skid, and the auto straightened out. Behind it, driven more slowly, were two more vehicles, a blocky Model T and the sleek length of a Packard. The Ford's loud engine droned stronger than the rushing wind.

"Ladies, please shut the door," Mrs. Bell urged.

"More guests, Mama." Clarrie peered around Nedda, squinting to see any detail through the pouring rain.

"Then fetch your brother and Little Tom." The lights of the entry flickered, and they all glanced at the ceiling-mounted light. Mrs. Bell's voice sounded calm as she added, "And tell your mama to start the generator."

A gust of wind carried soaking rain with it, and they retreated into the hall.

The dark touring auto drove past the steps and stopped with its chrome bumper in view. Little Tom, taller than Nedda, ran down the steps to help with luggage. In minutes he re-appeared with a young woman on his arm, hiding under a water-wilted newspaper. She dropped the newspaper on the porch, revealing a rain-flattened hat and soaked dress. Little Tom guided her up the steps then jumped down to reach the trunk. The woman waited on the porch, shivering, glancing between the auto and the shelter of the inn. Little Tom wrestled with something in the trunk only to have it removed from his hand.

Suitcase in hand, a tall man bounded up the steps and ushered the young woman inside as Hank and Paul came down the stairs, muffled in their slickers.

The man took off his Fedora and gave it a shake.

"Good Lord, it's Daddy," Flo exclaimed.

Hank stopped abruptly then stepped forward, extending his hand. "Sir. I didn't expect you."

"I'll not let my son marry without meeting the girl first. Florence, no child yet?"

"Not yet, Daddy." She drew Nedda's hand forward. "Here's our bride, Daddy. Miss Nedda Courtland. From England."

Paul reached his wife's side. "Sir," he said, but he didn't offer his hand.

Mr. McElroy Senior arched his brow. Ignoring the young woman clinging to his side, he gave Nedda a sweeping glance that judged her handkerchief frock and her simple jewelry, a beaded bracelet and dangling earrings. Harshly judged them, for he sneered. "Gold digger, Junior. Make sure nothing's in her name."

"She has twice my salary," Hank said smoothly. "She has shares in Ingram Investments."

That sharpened McElroy Senior's eyes, and he swept another look at her dress and green earrings. His eyes narrowed, for her earrings were clearly green glass, not emeralds. He snorted and turned away, commenting "Does she now?" That tone doubted his son's statement.

The girl beside him gave a little cough. "Henry," she whispered.

His expression changed, becoming an unctuous smile. "This is Dotty Moore." He added nothing more to explain her presence.

"How pleasant of you to come for Hank's wedding. I know he rang you, Daddy, but I did not know that he sent you an invitation to attend." Her gaze swept over Dotty. Flo nodded, too rude to ignore the young woman, then she turned to her husband. "Paul, I believe I will retire for a bit." He began shedding his slicker. "No, you help with the luggage. Not everyone who comes will be rattlers."

McElroy Senior laughed and moved for the hotel desk as his daughter removed herself from his presence. "Two rooms, side by side," he demanded.

A muted crash announced the loss of another tree branch from a live oak.

The Model T brought the Rev. and Mrs. Thomas, both soaked with rain that had swept through the glassless windows of their early-model vehicle.

"Creek's flooding," the Reverend informed them as he peeled out of his raincoat. "Only a foot below the bridge. This rain keeps up, we'll be cut off by morning. Would Little Tom move my old T, Clara? I dread contending with more rain."

"Excuse me, Mr. McElroy," the older woman said, "I'll be with you in a minute. You finish signing the register." She lifted a key from the board and slid it across the desk. "Room C, Third floor, Reverend. You and Mrs. Thomas hurry and dry off. I'll send Clarrie up with towels and hot tea. I'll sign you in myself." She rang the desk bell six times as her granddaughter dashed off. "Now, Mr. McElroy, if your friend will sign here and write her address below her name."

Little Tom carried in another light suitcase followed by a woman with an umbrella. Her twill raincoat and Mary Jane shoes were soaked. She dragged off her fisherman's hat as Hank started past her. Strawberry blonde hair fell free, refusing to remain in a sensible twist. A hairclip fell to the floor. "Oh bother! Hank McElroy, don't you dare ignore me. I want to meet your fiancée."

His scowl vanished. "Cat! You braved the rain. Nedda, come meet Cat Anderson."

The woman turned a freckled face to Nedda. Her washed blue eyes sparkled. She gave Hank a push. "Fetch my other suitcase, and I will forgive you for dragging me from Houston into a hurricane."

Nedda extended a hand which Cat immediately turned to examine the engagement ring. "Diamonds and a lovely emerald. Our small-town boy did good." She gave a baleful glance at the ceiling light. "That light is atrocious. But look at the sparkles. *Oo la la.*"

Without acknowledging McElroy Senior and his date still at the hotel desk, waiting for their keys, Cat drew Nedda into their vacated spot. Mrs. Bell handed them over, murmuring their room assignments, while Cat signed the ledger with a firm Spencerian *Catherine Anderson*. Giving Nedda no time to comment, she continued talking about the rain, the wind, and the mud until McElroy Senior and Miss Moore started up the stairs, following a Bell with their suitcase.

Cat glanced at the staircase then tapped the pen nib on McElroy's name. "I am surprised he tore himself away from his fishing. He'll have a reason. We don't pass and re-pass. Bad ton, as they say in those English society romances. My weakness. My brother's just like him. That's probably how he rooked Hank. Too nice for his own good. Do you read those society romances? I do believe I've found a new author. Careful with that, young man! It has the wedding gift. Did you say Room G, Mrs. Bell?"

"I did," Mrs. Bell said as Cat took a breath. Before the older woman could explain, Nedda seized her chance. "On the other end from me. First Floor, although you say Second Floor over here."

A half-hour later she had the gift of a silver frame engraved with tomorrow's date, "so Hank will never forget", and Cat had described much of Houston society and recommended two new novels for reading. "You'll need to meet Boone Galvin. He's TP&R's leading light. A widower for the past ten years. No interest in re-marriage so don't try to match him up. He will not appreciate it, and so he's told me many times. He drove me here. I never quite know how to take him. I think he's teasing me, but——. Well, you'll have to judge. And you'll need to watch out for my brother. I don't know how he convinced Hank to make him best man. He'll use that, too, I warrant, to turn into cash. He's my brother, but I know his faults."

When Hank later introduced the hard-jawed Boone Galvin, Nedda spotted the glint in his eyes when he watched Cat cross the room. Her new friend had missed the man's interest.

As Hank fetched their apertifs, Boone bent from his great height, inches more than Hank. "I had you investigated."

Nedda didn't pretend shock. "Should I worry? When did you send out the hounds?"

His wry smile crinkled his eyes. "When Mac reported a woman held two votes for Ingram Investments. Before the ruckus with the accountant."

"That early?"

"That early," he agreed.

"What do you think now?"

"You survived west Texas. More importantly, you survived a half-hour of Cat's chatter. You'll do."

"I like Cat," she sputtered in defense.

"So do I. Don't tell her, or she'll run for the hills, and I'll never catch her."

Nedda glanced up. He wasn't smiling, and the lack of expression exposed the paler skin inside his smile crinkles. He looked very serious, too serious for the flighty Cat—but then Cat wasn't really flighty. Her talk wrapped a lot of fluff around a core of wisdom. She nodded her agreement to maintain his secret.

Remembering Cat's talk of her brother, she looked around the parlor for Ray, but he remained absent until they gathered around the dining table, a cold repast of ham, deviled eggs, cucumbers tossed with thin-sliced onions in a vinaigrette, and a salad with olives and fresh tomatoes from the garden that the storm was destroying. Dessert was a thin slice of a lemon pie, a tart-sweet confection that Mrs. Bell called Poor Man's Pie. They were all complimenting Mrs. Bell when her husband stood from his place at the table's head.

"Ladies, men, you know that the hurricane is expected to make landfall south of Galveston. The wind and rain will be pretty bad for a while, but we should escape major damage. My wife and I think it wise if everyone sleeps here in the inn tonight. That means you two, Mr. and Mrs. Culpepper, and you, Mr. Stringer, and you, Mr. Phillips, will not stay in the cottages tonight. I'll send Junior and Eddie to carry any luggage you might want to bring over."

Mrs. Culpepper gave a dismayed cry.

"I do apologize, ma'am. Those oaks over the cottage have weathered many storms, but best be safe. You and your husband will be safer here in the inn."

The great crashing of a tree shuddered the inn and stopped any dissent.

"Will we have to share rooms?" someone asked.

"Mr. and Mrs. Culpepper will take the study, and we'll have the men in the parlor. I've some Army cots you can use."

"A cot! What about my back?" Mr. Stringer complained.

"You can try that Chesterfield," someone suggested.

"My wife will find sheets and pillows and blankets to make you as comfortable as possible. I know some of you stayed up talking until late, but tonight we'll call lights out at 10:30. We'll do the same tomorrow night if this hurricane's not well past us."

Mrs. Thomas, the reverend's wife, tutted. "Dear Miss Courtland, Mr. McElroy, I know a hurricane is the last thing you expected when you planned your wedding."

Nedda glanced down, thinking how little planning she'd actually done.

"We're flexible," Hank said. He clasped her hand under the table, his fingers warm and firm where hers were cold. "Rev. Thomas, how does that fit with you?"

"The benefit of retirement, Mr. McElroy, is that I have no pulpit obligations.. I can alter my plans to suit yours." He lifted his gaze to the ceiling as a muted crash revealed another tree lost to the storm.

Bootsteps in the hall had them turning to look. "Junior! Eddie!" Mr. Bell called.

His sons appeared, dressed in their slickers and gum boots.

"Where are you going, boys?"

"Bay's topped the dock, Dad."

Eddie cleared his throat. "These gentlemen may want to move their vehicles from under the trees. Park `em leeside of the kitchen." He'd barely finished speaking when chairs scraped back, men acting on his advice."

McElroy Senior tossed his keys to his son, who caught them on reflex. "Move my auto for me, Junior."

Hank didn't answer, but he dropped the keys in his pocket.

Mr. Bell followed the drivers. "Tom!" his wife called when she saw him drag on an overcoat. "You're too old to be hauling things about."

"I can oversee the parking, Clara. We don't want a mess behind the kitchen."

"It's getting dark, Tom. Take that big flashlight."

Henry McElroy, Al Rogers, and Ray Anderson followed him from the dining room. Mr. Phillips had gone to move Mr. Rogers' auto, confirming Nedda's guess that the silent man obeyed the club owner.

The women gathered plates and tea glasses. "What about your sons' wives and the children?" Flo asked. "Don't they live in the cottages?"

"Bless you, dear. They'll be in the cellar tonight, all warm and cozy. I doubt the boys will sleep until the storm's passed over. Stack the plates here, ladies." She set the ham platter on a rough table in the short hall to the back door. Her husband had left the big door open, and the screened door drifted open and shut as the wind gusted around the inn then roared inland.

Nedda peeked out the back door. The day had darkened to a deeper twilight although the sun wouldn't set for another half-hour. In the hour of dinner the winds had shifted to a straight gale, forcing passage against the inn's stout walls. The wind forced the tree limbs to reach inland. Leaves and small branches littered the sodden lawn. The kitchen garden looked raked over, fruiting plants jerked onto the ground. Dark bits tumbled through the air, torn away so quickly that she couldn't identify them.

Motors started. Mr. Bell swung the flashlight, the beam bright as it lanced through the driving rain. He directed the vehicles in a line behind the long kitchen building.

A draft caught the screen and ripped it open. Nedda dragged it shut and jerked it hard to stick within the wet jamb. Then she retreated.

Two ladies stacked bowls onto plates. Mrs. Bell appeared in a slicker, as did Flo and Cat, descending the staircase together. "We're taking the plates over," Flo said. "Those little girls don't need to come out in the rain."

"I'll help," and Nedda hurried for her coat.

When she opened her door to leave her room, buttoning the Bombazine that Hank insisted she buy, she heard two men talking nearby. She peeked out, but something kept her planted on her room's carpet.

"Not going to work," one man said, sounding very certain.

"Anderson assures me——."

"You trust the word of that lousy gambler?"

In the heavy silence of that question, Nedda inched back. She didn't want to be seen.

"I made promises. I can't go back on them."

Her mind raced. *Who were these two?* One had to be Al Rogers. The other wasn't Ray Anderson. Besides, Mr. Rogers had referred to Ray. Not him then. *Was he McElroy Senior?*

The other man snorted. "He can't pressure Junior," and that confirmed the man for Nedda. "My son's wise to him now. He won't find it so easy to coerce him as he did five years ago. Anderson blew his chance with Junior."

That sounded like both men needed Hank to do something, and they needed Ray to persuade him.

She remembered the three arguments Hank had had with Ray. All had left Hank disgruntled and not wanting to talk and unwilling to share.

Her fists clenched. The engagement ring bit into her fingers.

"You have a better idea, McElroy?"

"I have my ways."

"Look, we can't talk out here." A flash, rainbow sparkled, for light must have caught that big diamond on Rogers' pinkie finger. "They'll be back soon. Come in here."

She waited until the door shut before she stepped into the now-empty hall and eased her door shut.

And locked it.

. ~ . ~ . ~ .

The storm strengthened before midnight, skirling above them. The inn creaked in the unrelenting gale. As the building swayed and groaned, those still awake decided to shift to downstairs.

They knocked on doors to share the plan. Only a few remained in their rooms.

Ray sloshed his whiskey bottle in Nedda's face. "Here's my comfort."

McElroy Senior decided for Dotty that they would remain in their rooms.

Al Rogers glared then slammed his door.

Pearl Lawrence yawned as she dragged a pretty floral wrapper over her shoulder but shook her head, determining to ride out the night. "Safer than Galveston," she judged.

They took blankets and pillows and trooped downstairs to shelter in the hall. By common consent, they gave the settee across from the hotel desk to Rev. and Mrs. Thomas. Flo and Paul bundled together, whispering a little before she burrowed her head against her husband. Cat marched to the wall outside the study and glared at Boone when he started to follow her. Colfax rolled into his blanket, punched his pillow a few times, then dropped to sleep. Hank used his blanket for a pad and tossed Nedda's over both of them. He jammed his pillow against hers but left her enough room that she wasn't crowded against the wall. He draped an arm over her waist and fell asleep with a quickness she envied. She watched the shadows cast by the flickering oil lantern for a long time.

Only to rouse as Hank settled beside her. "What? Where?"

"Hush."

"Where did you go?"

"Checking on things."

She accepted it and closed her eyes, but memory of the slammed door refused to be quiet. "I refuse to help Mr. Rogers," she whispered.

Hank shook with laughter. "Sleep."

"Alright," she said drowsily.

But she was awake now, and sleep would have to be coaxed to return. She thought over tomorrow, over the wedding to come, and a glow started through her. From the very first Hank had gone out of his way to help. Protector wasn't a guise he donned; the instinct wore deep into his being.

Checking on things.

She watched him until drowsiness returned and cast her back into sleep.

3 ~ Die

The straight-line gale remained steady through the wee hours.

Hank, Paul, and Boone used flashlights to check around the inn, keeping to the porches back and front. The pines had bent with the wind, pitiful rather than proud sentinels of the road. Three more oaks had crashed down. The flashlight beam highlighted the nearest cottage destroyed by the massive branch of a live oak. Then the rain became torrential, obscuring the damage.

The bay had risen far beyond its shore. In the night it crept high onto the lawn, lapping against Mrs. Bell's round garden that centered the turn-around. It came no higher. When the tide ebbed, the storm surge lowered with it.

Although dappled with storm litter, the automobiles behind the kitchen had taken no damage. The storm drove the men inside before they could assess any damage to the other cottages. The torrential rain became fitful then resumed its deluge.

The air inside the closed-up inn became stifling. They agreed to open the back door. On the leeside of the inn, no wind would rush in, and the porch protected the door from the rain. The stifling air dissipated, hastened by a strong draft. The stuffy air of the hallway cooled and almost became comfortable.

Dawn enabled them to see beyond the inn's immediate surroundings.

The ruined cottage had crumpled beneath the oak. Green-trimmed white walls had splintered and broken under the massive weight. Limbs had damaged another cottage's roof and broken a porch of a third cottage. Clean-up would take weeks.

Hank and Paul ventured further out and reported that the planked bridge had survived. The creek had piled debris against it and water still flowed over it, but it looked sturdy on its supports. "Might take full morning for the creek to subside," Paul judged, wiping water from his face and accepting the black coffee Flo had brewed in the back hall.

Tom Bell fired up the generator again, restoring the electrics. The ceiling fans swept around the air, and it seemed less stuffy, just wet.

Their stirring about had awakened Mr. Stringer and Mr. Phillips, who both came to the hall, rumpled from their night on old Army cots. Mr. Culpepper emerged from the study yet closed the door behind him, giving his wife longer privacy.

Mrs. Bell turned on the radio. Hearing only static, she lowered the volume to a low crackle.

"Telephone's still out," Clarrie reported.

Mrs. Bell hmphed, unruffled by the grumbles of thunder. "We have electrics. We have everything we stocked for this weekend. The girls and I will prepare a quick breakfast. If you don't mind a great change, Miss Courtland, I suggest Rev. Thomas perform your wedding at noon. We'll have the dinner after."

The offer surprised Nedda. She glanced to Hank for his reaction.

"You'll be wanting to work on the storm debris," he guessed.

"We're well stocked, but some people may want to leave as soon as we can confirm the roads into Baytown."

Mrs. Thomas clutched her worn flannel robe tight to her neck. "How will we confirm the roads? Jefferson?"

"I imagine a deputy will check on the Back Bay. Is that right, Mr. Bell?"

The older man grunted assent. "Once the bridge isn't in flood, we still need to know the state of the roads. Gets low in there just past the bridge. The bay will have washed over that, I reckon. We'll sit tight until a deputy gives us the all-clear."

Mr. Phillips shouldered between Cat and the wall, intent on reaching the stairs. Her "Sir?" iced him.

"Need to talk to my boss," he gruffed and made for the stairway, still in darkness. He stubbed a toe on one of the steps but continued upward, his feet heavy as he climbed one flight then the other.

The reverend turned to Nedda. "Miss Courtland, the storm has thrown out all your wedding plans. We should have had a rehearsal last evening, but I vow that was the last thing on my mind."

Hank grasped her hand and gave it a little kiss above the ring. "Everyone we need is here. What do you want to do? We can delay the ceremony and have it in Houston, or we can stick to the plan for this evening. Or we can say our vows at noon and celebrate all afternoon. We weren't planning to leave until Monday."

She squeezed his fingers. "Mr. Bell, do you think the deputy will arrive before noon?"

"Real emergencies will have the sheriff's attention, miss. Here in Back Bay, we didn't get the brunt of the storm surge. This morning the Sheriff's Office will have their hands full with the people around Baytown."

"Mrs. Bell, will you need any help to have things ready for after a noontime ceremony?"

"Bless you, Miss Courtland, that's no trouble at all, as long as we start preparing now."

Nedda looked up at Hank. "Noon is a lovely time for a wedding, and this storm will provide us with a unique story of our wedding day."

Rev. Thomas cleared his throat. "Mr. McElroy, Miss Courtland, if we could briefly discuss the ceremony."

"You don't need me for this," Cat said and started for the stairs. "I'll tag along behind Flo. I'll wake Ray. I can't believe he slept the night through. Up on the third floor, that wind would have roared, not been muffled like down here. I'll send Ray down."

Boone Galvin shoved his empty coffee cup at Hank. "I'll head up, too."

Rev. Thomas led them to the parlor.

Although he edged out of the doorway, Mr. Stringer looked affronted at their invasion. He tossed his blanket over his cot and plopped down on it.

The reverend ignored his huffiness and gave an expansive wave of his arm. "We'll have the front window open. If I judge my time aright, the worst of the storm should be well past us by mid-morning. Miss Courtland, who will escort you to the altar?" He patted the marble-topped console table between the two large windows, still shuttered against the wind.

"I will," Colfax said. "We're like family, Nedda. I should do it."

She beamed, and he gave a sheepish grin.

"Bride here, with your ladies behind you," Rev. Thomas indicated a medallion on the carpet, "and groom and best man and groomsman here, supporting you, Mr. McElroy."

Rapid footsteps descended the stairs. "That will be Ray."

But Ray Anderson didn't appear in the parlor doorway. Boone did. "Anderson's missing."

"What?"

Cat came behind Boone, her face so pale that the freckles stood out. "Missing. Gone. Absent. Vanished." Her voice trembled, but her cloud-colored eyes glittered with anger. "My brother is not in his room. He *has* been to bed. He's not there now. I have no idea where he is."

"But where--?"

"Exactly," she snapped.

"There's water on the floor at his window, and wet foot tracks from window to door," Boone explained. "Looked like he opened his window during the storm then shut it back."

"He's on a bender." Cat cast her eyes upward. "I warned you, Hank."

"You did. Well, Ray's lost his chance. As Nedda said, we're adaptable. Paul, will you step up as best man?"

"Glad to do it."

"Boone, I'm short a groomsman. Would you escort Cat?"

The tall man glanced at her. "She's spitting like a cat. As long as she doesn't bring out her claws—" Cat narrowed her eyes and hissed. He chuckled. "—like that. Happy to do so, Mac. How long will your beauty treatments take, Cat? You may need to get started."

"Oh, you!" She swatted his arm, but his teasing had killed her temper at her brother.

The reverend cleared his throat. "Then we have only the vows themselves. I am inclined to use the ceremony from the Book of Common Prayer." Then he lifted his head. "Listen! I do believe the wind has stopped."

They all listened. The inn's creaks and crackings had stopped. No crashes came from downed limbs. Then the wind resumed, but no longer did it roar.

. ~ . ~ . ~ .

By the end of the satisfying wedding luncheon, the sun blazed onto the sodden landscape as the last clouds scubbed away. Only tattered streamers lagged behind.

After the obligatory photos of the bridal party and guests, Cat exclaimed that the best photos would have the bay in the background. "Look, the water's still choppy. All those whitecaps will show wonderfully well on film."

They posed several yards in front of the upturned dinghies. The land by the boats remained too sodden for the ladies to navigate in their heels. The waves billowed behind the dinghies. Their blue and red and yellow paint and the gleaming dark varnish of the canoe made Nedda wish the camera had colored film.

They had a view of the storm's destruction, fallen trees and the crushed cottage, but people who viewed the photographs would not see that destruction.

The putter of an engine alerted them to a Model T navigating the muddy road, veering around downed pines. As it turned toward the inn, it came into full view. Painted on the driver door was a white badge, proclaiming *Chambers County Sheriff*. Colfax ran inside to alert Mr. Bell while the men of the wedding party walked back to the turn-around.

The deputy cut the engine and climbed out. The wheels of the Model T were mud-mortared, and bits of debris marked the waterline of a flood the deputy had driven through. The man was stocky, with a face burned by the sun. He shaded his eyes to study the bridal party, the men nearby while the women stood back. He turned to survey the damaged cottage.

Hank broke the silence of birdsong and gusting wind. "Afternoon, deputy. We didn't know the flood had receded from the bridge."

"Road's still flooded aways back. Looks like the old inn suffered no damage. Anybody in that cottage?"

"No. The Bells ordered everyone to the inn before the hurricane struck."

He surveyed the women with Nedda in her champagne-colored gown while Flo and Cat wore matching handkerchief frocks in turquoise and tulle. "Havin' a party?"

"A wedding."

"Ah, that would be where Rev. Thomas and his wife went. Don't see his auto."

"It's parked behind the kitchen. All of our vehicles are there."

"That's good. Didn't lose any to storm damage?"

"We have Mr. Bell to thank for that." Hank took a few forward steps and thrust out his hand. "I'm Hank McElroy. This is Paul Jackson, my best man, and Boone Galvin, my groomsman."

"Galvin," the deputy drawled as he shook Boone's hand. "You with the oil people?"

"I am. We all are."

"Family concern?"

"Friends. Formed the company after the war."

"Deputy, come meet my bride."

The man was willing although he glanced at the inn where their host now stood on the porch. "Be with you in a jiffy, Mr. Bell."

When Hank introduced "my bride, the new Mrs. McElroy," happiness shimmered through Nedda.

Colfax jumped down the steps to rejoin them.

Cat insisted on taking the deputy's photograph," and you must have cake."

Yet he wasn't listening. He squinted at the dinghies dragged onto the lawn. "Is that a shoe? And a man's hand." He strode to the boats.

The men followed. Flo gasped then clapped a hand over her mouth. "We were just standing, taking pictures."

Nedda glanced at Cat, for only one person had gone missing.

"My brother Ray," Cat said and began to close the Brownie. Her hands shook. She nearly dropped the camera. Flo took it from her and folded it away.

Hank and Boone flipped over a yellow dinghy to reveal the body.

Ray Anderson lay awkwardly on rain-soaked ground. The deputy knelt and shut his eyes. He plucked red and orange petals and green leaves from Ray's soaked clothes. When the flattened grass swished as Paul walked away, he looked around. "Here, where you goin'?"

Paul pointed at the tracks in the grass, faint indentations in a clear angle to the front façade of the inn. He followed spot to spot. In taking photographs, they had walked over some of the marks. Closer to the inn, the drag lines to the yellow dinghy were evident—once they knew to look for them. The gravel in the turn-around showed disturbance. Crushed and flattened flowers aligned with Ray's room above.

He had tumbled off the porch into the flowerbed.

"Drunk," Cat said bitterly. "I said drink would be the death of him."

"Then who moved his body?" Boone asked, voice quiet but cold with logic. "Who flipped the dinghy over to hide him? That's intent."

"His neck's broken," Hank added.

"Somebody throttled him," the deputy said. "Marks on his neck. Mr. Bell, I'll trouble you for a couple of sheets." The old man hurried to obey.

"Might be best to put the man in the cellar. And ma'am, if I could bother you to take some photos."

At the request, Cat looked like she would throw up. "I'll do it," Paul said, and his wife put the Brownie camera in his hand.

"How will you inform the sheriff?"

"Can't, with all the wires down. I ain't leavin' until the sheriff tells me what to do. When I don't report in, he'll come lookin'. Until then, well, we'll see what we can see."

4 ~ Suspects

Deputy Hicks had a straightforward method. He plodded one step after another and didn't jump ahead. That process worked for some problems, but flexibility occasionally was necessary.

Flexibility was necessary now.

Keeping Ray's body cold was Hicks' top priority. He focused on the Bell brothers carrying the body in a sling formed of sheets. Preserving the dinghy location was second. He appointed Little Tom to monitor the site until he could inspect it.

"Ray's room," Nedda whispered to Hank. "If there's any evidence there—."

"Which was the victim's room?" Hicks asked Mrs. Bell.

"Third Floor, Room E. Above where he landed."

"All the rooms can access the porch?"

"Only the three on the front."

"Could he have dropped from the second-story porch?"

Nedda flinched at the question, realizing how Ray's neck became broken.

"Ray's window had to be opened during the storm," Boone offered. "The floor and carpet at the window are soaked."

"You saw that?" The deputy's eyes gleamed.

"His sister and I checked on Ray when he didn't come down this morning. The shutters and window must have been unlocked. They are locked now."

"And his bed was slept in," Cat added.

"He had on regular clothes," Paul pointed out. "Maybe his bed was rumpled to look like he'd slept in it."

"We can tell that soon enough." Hicks turned to Mrs. Bell. "I'd like to see his room then all the rooms on the front, third and second floors."

She fetched a master key.

"You should note where we were," Nedda huffed. Investigations were slow; she wanted this one to be over and done with. "Most of us were here in the hall through the night. We know Ray was alive when we came down."

"How do you know that, Mrs. McElroy?"

"He shook his whiskey bottle in my face, Deputy."

"That's how we know he was drunk," Cat added. "Everyone in the hall, we can alibi each other. And Mr. Stringer and Mr. Phillips and the Culpeppers, they were in the parlor and the study. We would have seen them go upstairs."

A motor revved, rumbling loud and louder.

For a second everyone stood frozen, then Hank and Paul broke free of shock and ran to the back hall. The screen door slammed, sharp as a pistol shot. The deputy followed, also letting the screen strike the frame.

Boone withdrew a leather-covered notebook from an inner jacket pocket. He swiped the pen at the hotel ledger and began writing, spelling aloud "Culpeppers. Stringer. Phillips. Cat. Me. Paul and Flo. Hank and Nedda. Colfax."

"And the Bells," Flo bit out. Ray's body had killed her joy in the wedding. She had her arms crossed, hugging herself as if chilled although the coolness briefly restored with the hurricane had vanished. "They were in their room, and their sons and their families were in the cellar."

"That's everyone with an alibi we can trust," Nedda said.

The auto engine ceased. They watched the back door, but the men didn't miraculously appear with the murderer.

"Henry McElroy," Cat ticked off on her fingers, "Dotty Moore, Al Rogers, Pearl Lawrence."

"I think we can eliminate the women," Boone said, adding their names to his list. "They wouldn't have been strong enough to overpower Anderson."

"He was drunk, really drunk," Cat reminded. "But you're right. They wouldn't have the strength in their hands. Not at all. And they certainly were not strong enough to lift him over the porch railing—."

"Don't! How can you describe—? He's your brother! I know you two had your arguments, but—that's heartless, Cat!"

She stared at Flo then looked away, her throat working. Boone reached a hand to her, but she pushed him away. "No. Don't—. No!" She spun and ran upstairs. They heard her sob as she reached the top.

Nedda started after her.

"No," Boone said.

"But—."

"No. She needs to cry, and she won't countenance anyone seeing that," he explained. "She needs the world to think she's strong and emotionless. That's how her parents taught her to be. Tears are a weakness you don't show an enemy."

"I'm not an enemy! I'm her friend, a new friend, that I grant you, but still—."

"We'll leave her alone for a little while," Flo advised, "then we'll both go to her. And Boone Galvin, who had your raising? Tears and weakness and enemies? About Cat?"

He shrugged. "I know who had her raising. That's how they would consider it. Mr. Stringer, I thought you were in the parlor."

"I heard my name." He canted an odd look at Boone. "You were narrowing the suspect list."

"Why are you here, Mr. Stringer?" Nedda asked. "A quick vacation after the families with children have ended their holidays to resume school."

"Sure," he agreed. "Bachelors avoid families with children. I would be hunting gators today except for the hurricane."

"Only you are not a bachelor, are you? Your wedding band left a strong tan line."

He looked at his ring finger with the tell-tale paler line of a ring. Then he grinned, affable as yesterday afternoon when he'd regaled her with tales of gambling and speakeasies in Galveston. He dug into his pocket and brought out a gold circle which he returned to his finger. "Call this weekend a bachelor weekend while my wife takes the children to visit their grandparents."

"You never told me your profession."

"This and that."

"Stringer," Boone said slowly. "I know that name."

"We've never met," the man said quickly.

"No, we haven't. I would remember that."

"He talked about Galveston," Nedda supplied. "Luck and the ladies. Luck with cards? Are you friends with Mr. Rogers?"

"Friends, no."

"Did you come to meet him? To spy on him?"

"No, no. I don't gamble."

Flo looked up from the hotel ledger. "Cicero Stringer, Texas Avenue, Houston. That's an unusual name. And Texas Avenue. Isn't the *Houston Post* on that street?"

Boone snapped his fingers. "That's it. Newspaper man. Were you following us?"

"Look, when three of the top men in Texas Petroleum & Refining come to one destination, that's news. Oil is big news."

"They came for a wedding," Nedda cut in.

"My editor didn't know that. And the story's gotten bigger. Murder during a hurricane. A wedding. With wildcatters of the oil industry involved. And a Galveston club owner. Add in two scarlet women, and everyone will buy my story. So, since you've cottoned to me, you might as well know that Phillips, the boxer, he left the parlor last night. He went out the window."

"You didn't tell anyone that Phillips left?"

"What did it matter to me? Nobody knew Ray Anderson was dead. Or about to be dead. You think Phillips killed him?"

"Where did he go, Stringer?"

"Up the back porch stair."

"There's a back porch stair?" Flo shot in.

"Yep. Goes all the way to the top. My guess is he went to check on his boss Al Rogers. Phillips is his heavy, you know."

"I had surmised that." Boone tapped the pen on his list then crossed out Phillips' name. "We're to three suspects then."

"But what would be the motive?" Flo turned back a ledger page. "Ray came here with Mr. Rogers."

I made promises, Nedda remember the club owner swearing, *I can't go back on them.*

And he'd called Ray a *lousy gambler.*

Rogers and McElroy Senior had that conversation, with her as an unexpected eavesdropper. What was the cliché? Eavesdroppers never hear good of themselves. She'd heard something concerning Hank. His father had said, *Anderson blew his chance with Junior.*

What chance?

Oil is big news, Stringer said, and he'd followed three of the top men at TP&R because he sniffed after a story.

Ray had brought Al Rogers.

McElroy Senior had shown up, not invited to the wedding but not uninvited either. He claimed he had to be there for his son. And he plotted with Al Rogers. They were using Ray to coerce Hank.

Coerce him to do what?

Oil.

Oil was big money now and promised to be even bigger money.

Promises. I can't go back on them.

Before Nedda sorted everything in her mind, men's raised voices grew louder. A clatter of steps on the back porch, then Hank hustled Henry McElroy into the back hall. Paul carried two suitcases. Dotty Moore clutched her train case like a shield. Deputy Hicks walked behind them.

As soon as they reached the main hall, Hank snatched his hand away from his father. "This idiot—."

"Junior!"

"You're an idiot, Dad, no two ways about it. He was going to leave, he and Dotty."

"I didn't want to go," the young woman cried.

Paul dropped the suitcases. One toppled over. "If the ground hadn't been saturated, they'd be gone. Now his auto is mired to the wheel hub."

"Wedding's over," McElroy Senior said. "No reason to stay. You're a sweet lady, Nedda, but I've places to be. I can't waste time here."

"You leave just when we find Ray Anderson's dead body. That looks more than suspicious, Dad. What will that deputy think? Did you think he'd stand around twiddling his thumbs while you left? He's looking for Ray's murderer!"

"I didn't kill Ray!"

"Deputy Hicks can't rely on your word alone. He needs proof."

"Dotty will alibi me."

"Oh, sure, he's going to believe a pr—."

"Don't you say it, Junior."

"Then I'll say this. Hicks has no reason to trust you and no reason to trust her. What do you think your leaving would look like? Flight. You're a suspect in a murder, and you decide to run."

"I tell you, I didn't kill Ray!"

"We need evidence, Dad. Your word won't hold in a court of law. Not after that charge of fraud three years ago."

"That wasn't fraud!"

"The district attorney filed charges."

"And the judge dropped them."

"Who did you buy off?" Flo snapped.

"What?"

"Who did you buy off? Who did you bribe?" She faced her father with crossed arms and a scowl that would have terrified Nedda had it bent her way. "That's the way you always work, isn't it? The gossip I've heard—. If it's not a bribe, it's blackmail."

Bribery. Blackmail. Secrets.

"You've room to talk," her father snapped. "You think I don't know—."

"I think," Deputy Hicks' twang cut across the dispute. "We need to settle down. Where were you going to go, sir?"

"No reason to stay," McElroy Senior said, sullen. "I'm only here for the wedding. That's over. Bridge is clear. Dotty and I can leave."

"Not without the sheriff's approval."

"You can give that."

"No, sir. No, I can't. Don't have the authority. You have to wait for the sheriff's approval."

"That could take hours!"

"Then we wait hours. Gives me time to investigate this here murder. Is that the reason you were all-fired to hurry? You wanted gone before I investigated?"

"I'll stay. But Dotty and I will leave as soon as you clear us."

"*After* you *pay* Mr. Bell, not before." Muffled footsteps started their descent. Hicks cocked his head to listen then spread his arm. "Why don't you all head to the dining room? Mr. Bell can give you lemonade and cake, can't you, Mr. Bell?" He turned to the stairs. "Mr. Rogers, you and Phillips can go in there, too. We missing anyone?"

"Miss Lawrence," Stationed at the desk, her eyes darting from speaker to speaker, Mrs. Bell spoke up quickly. "I'll send Clarrie to fetch her. Do you want my family in the dining room, too?"

"No, ma'am. I think we can all agree that Mr. Anderson was unknown to y'all before his arrival on Wednesday. Unless one of your boys went off his head, they didn't have nothing to do with this murder. I get all your guests in one room—well, you can monitor yourselves while I investigate."

"Um, excuse me, please, Deputy. May I change from this gown?" Nedda flicked the gossamer skirt. "I'm certain Flo—Mrs. Jackson would like to change as well. And we will see to it that Miss Anderson will change and return with us."

Hicks looked at Flo then sighed. "Miss Anderson?"

"Ray's sister. She … needed a little privacy."

"Oh. I remember. Red hair." He looked nonplussed. "And we're still missing Miss Lawrence. Which of you have rooms on the back, with the porch stairs?"

Flo raised her hand. "Both Cat and I do."

"And that Miss Lawrence?"

"She does," Mrs. Bell confirmed.

"You get that Miss Lawrence down here. Send your daughters-in-law to watch these ladies. One in the hall, one on the porch; that should do it."

"We can change?" That brightened Nedda's slump. Not only could she preserve this gown from further wear, but alone, she would have time to think.

Before she started upstairs, she sidled over to Boone. Hank frowned, but Boone merely raised his eyebrows. She whispered, "Mr. Stringer and Mr. Phillips in the parlor last night—."

"Yes?"

"If Mr. Phillips left with only Mr. Stringer knowing, then Mr. Stringer also could have left."

"You're right. You're very right." He opened his notebook and circled Stringer's name.

5 ~ Revelation

Nedda fluffed the skirt of her wedding gown, checking that the shimmering lace had no pulls or tears. The pale champagne gold undergown looked as fragile as the lace, as wondrously created, fine as gossamer silk.

As fragile as life. As wondrously made as a person.

Fearfully and wonderfully made.

With all his faults, Ray Anderson was a creation of God, "a piece of work" as Hamlet said, wonderfully made but wholly corrupted by greed, by petty selfishness, by a hidden wrath against people he called friends— for he used them for his own gain. That wasn't friendship.

Contradictory emotions tore at Ray's sister Cat. She grieved for her brother, for the one she'd loved as a child, yet she had to be relieved that his lies and manipulations would not continue.

Who hated him enough to murder him?

Al Rogers? Henry McElroy? Both had reason to kill. Ray had somehow betrayed Rogers, who would break risky promises because Ray fell through on a plan. McElroy Senior worked with Rogers. He hadn't promised, but the backlash would catch him.

Which one had killed Ray?

Or had Phillips killed Ray on Rogers' order?

Were all three complicit? Or had one killed while the other two knew nothing?

Rogers said Anderson knew secrets that Hank didn't want exposed. Ray could easily have secrets on Rogers, on McElroy, on others.

And Ray's secrets about Hank?

Nedda didn't want to contemplate that level of evil in the man she loved. Yet he'd left the hallway last night. She had awakened on his return, not when he left. He'd dismissed her question about where he'd gone. Had he killed his best man?

What am I going to do? Do I tell Deputy Hicks about Ray's coercion attempts? If pressed, if backed into a corner, Rogers will tell Hicks about Hank, about Ray's blackmail. Blackmail was evil. *And murder is more than evil.*

Had Hank committed murder?

There, I've said it. Did he?

She couldn't reconcile it with the man she loved.

What am I going to do?

. ~ . ~ . ~ .

When Nedda returned with Flo and Cat, the Bell women following them down the stairway, Deputy Hicks had left the dining room, off with Mr. Bell.

The Culpeppers whispered together. Nedda found herself looking at Mr. Culpepper's long thin fingers, knotted with the early stages of arthritis. She remembered him rowing along the bay. The size of the oars would have fit his hands, not requiring him to do more than curl his fingers over the thick oars. Had Ray blackmailed him? Or Mrs. Culpepper? A blackmailer could ruin both people in a marriage, sucking them dry of money and hope. Had Mr. Culpepper killed Ray?

McElroy Senior stared out the window, gaze distant and unfocused. Dotty Moore clung to her seat, her lips rigid with fear.

At the head of the table, Mr. Bell's rightful place, Al Rogers talked with Mr. Stringer. The reporter jotted in his notepad, flipping to the next page. It sounded like they compared notes about an event in Galveston.

She slipped onto a chair between Mr. Stringer and Hank. Flo spoke quietly to her husband. Boone started a one-sided conversation with Cat; she didn't answer him, but she nodded and shook her head at the right places. Colfax sat in the corner, flipping through a glossy magazine.

Nedda slipped her hand over to Hank, and he quickly enveloped it. Did she wait for Deputy Hicks to blunder through his investigation and expose secrets unnecessarily, or ask her own questions that might give the right answers? She steeled herself to accept whatever backlash resulted. "Mr. McElroy?"

He startled and turned his head on a stiff pivot.

"Sir, why did you come here?"

"Nedda—."

McElroy spoke over Hank. "I told you, I wasn't going to miss my son's wedding."

"And were you going to apply pressure on him?" Conversation stopped. Nedda didn't look around the table. She knew that question attracted dangerous attention, but she wouldn't withdraw it.

"Pressure?" McElroy chuffed. "What can I force a grown man like my son to do? I haven't had any control over him since before the war."

Her heart began racing with fear that she'd misinterpreted what she'd heard, but she threw out the words, building the cage of her evidence. "Yet you did assure Mr. Rogers that Ray would be able to manipulate Hank."

A vein ticked in his temple. Tendons in his neck tightened and stood out. Rather than fear his obvious anger, his reaction steadied her. It served as proof that she'd guessed rightly. "That's none of your business, woman."

She gave a little smile. "Is it not? Whose business? Mr. Rogers' business?" Only then did she look at Al Rogers.

He wore another of his sleek suits, navy with a bold orange pinstripe, echoed by the orange silk handkerchief in his pocket. He'd unbuttoned his jacket when he sat, and Nedda fancied that she could see the tumultuous beat of his heart where the navy lapels revealed his silk shirt. "You back right on out of that," he gritted.

Her blow had struck both men. "Should I?" She lifted her chin and glared back at Rogers.

Phillips pushed back his chair. Hank loosed her hand and leaned forward.

"No," Rogers snapped. His gaze cut to his heavy. The boxer eased back in his chair. Hank remained leant forward, his arm on the table, ready to block Phillips.

The others had silenced, glancing from Nedda to Mr. Rogers, occasionally to Mr. McElroy. Mr. Culpepper, on Rogers' other side, had blanched. His wife cowered in her chair. Paul watched Rogers, but Flo's narrowed eyes were on her father. She never looked away from him. Mr. Stringer had flinched. Now he looked at his notes on Galveston, running his finger along the sewn binding of his notebook. At the foot of the table, Rev. Thomas held his handkerchief to his mouth. His hand shook. Mrs. Thomas looked a little lost, a little angry, tired and losing the thread.

Boone had stuck a finger in his jacket pocket; Nedda wondered if he had a weapon. She should have brought her purse with the Webley.

And Cat looked lost.

"Yes," Nedda said softly, "I believe you three had a conspiracy. You, Mr. McElroy, and Ray. You came to the wedding, both of you, to ensure Ray forced Hank into a corner."

McElroy laughed. The sound had no mirth. "Conspiracy! We're not in business together."

Rogers didn't try to laugh away Nedda's claim. "How do you figure that, ma'am?" His voice was all politeness, but his eyes—oh, his eyes held flames.

"I did hear your conversation with Mr. McElroy."

"We spoke in his room," he flashed back.

He'd just admitted they spoke privately, the first step in admitting to the conspiracy. Gently she pointed out, "You spoke in the hall to begin with. That's what I heard. Ray was to coerce Hank into doing something. And you did warn me, on Thursday, that Hank might have secrets I would not want to know."

"You've got grit, lady. That's dangerous."

"Oh my," Rev. Thomas said. He dabbed his mouth. "Dear Mrs. McElroy, ask no more. Please, I beg you. This is not a good man."

She ignored Rogers' covert threat and Rev. Thomas' plea. "I ask myself what you could want from Hank, you and Mr. McElroy and Ray, all three together, all three from different places, with different directions in your lives."

"Not so different."

The fire remained in his steady gaze, but she no longer feared it would scorch her. "The only thing I can name is an association with Texas P & R."

"Like a stake in the company. Bite into the controlling shares," Boone said. "We took thirds, 33% each, but someone had to take 34%. Hank lost the coin toss."

Hand fisted on the table, Paul gave the next step. "And when Anderson applied his thumb screws to snare 20%, Hank refused. Yep, he told us what Anderson said. My apologies, Cat."

"Don't apologize. I know what my brother was. I'm learning he was worse."

"We backed Hank," Boone added. "We backed him up over in France. I don't know what Anderson thought he had over on Hank. It doesn't matter now."

"No wonder Ray got drunk," Cat murmured. "Idiot."

Nedda returned to her questions. "What hold did you have on Ray, Mr. Rogers?"

His gaze slewed from Cat to her. Then he rested against the back of his chair, one hand relaxing on the table, the diamond on his little finger flashing. That hand didn't look tainted with blood. "Anderson said that Hank only needed a bit more convincing. The man was a smooth liar, and I knew it. I told McElroy it wouldn't work." He turned those fiery eyes on McElroy Senior.

The man sputtered. "It would work; it *would*. If Anderson threatened to tell this gold digger—."

"I told you, Dad, she's not a gold digger."

McElroy shrugged. "She's after your money. She has to be."

"Because you are?"

Nedda ignored the dispute. "Mr. Rogers, do you know where Pearl Lawrence is?"

Mr. Stringer dropped his notebook. With a mutter he dove under the table to pick it up.

Mrs. Culpepper coughed. "I saw her. After the wedding luncheon, before that deputy came. She was leaving. She had her suitcase, and she was walking into the woods behind the cottages."

Mr. Stringer climbed into his seat, but he had pushed away from the table, sitting behind Nedda, out of her line of sight. *Now,* she thought with a wry amusement, *now he's worried about sitting near Al Rogers.*

"That's curious," Flo mused. "Why would Miss Lawrence leave? She couldn't commit the murder. I'm sorry, Cat. We're talking about your brother—."

"Who got himself killed," she said bluntly although a tear dropped from her glimmering eyes. She wiped it away with a rough hand. "I'd rather have all this now than have to hear it for the first time in a courtroom. We all know Ray had a cluster of flaws, but I never thought he would try to blackmail a friend."

"He tried bribery first," Hank said quietly. His eyes dropped to the table. "He offered a clear $50,000 for the shares and a spot on the company board. I'm not certain he knew I am on the board."

"Chairman," Paul muttered.

"$50,000!" Mr. Culpepper whistled.

"Ray didn't have that kind of cash," Cat protested.

"Mr. Rogers?" Nedda asked.

"Money didn't come into my part of it. I know someone who could offer that much, though."

"I offered it." McElroy bit out, angry that his plan to cheat his son had fallen apart. "That was to be my payment to Anderson when he turned over the shares."

"Which you and Mr. Rogers would then sell?"

"You answer her," Rogers drawled. "You handled that part of it."

"Yes. Alright, yes, you've worked it out. Proud of yourself?"

"Who was the buyer?" Boone asked.

A door opened in the hall. Someone entered from the porch and rang the desk bell.

"Does it matter?" McElroy had deflated with the admission. "The chance is lost now."

"A syndicate, perhaps."

"Mafia?" Paul exchanged dire glances with Boone and Hank. "That's trouble." Boone muttered a word that Nedda didn't catch. She caught a glance at Colfax in the corner, on the edge of his seat and drinking in every word.

Loud voices started in the hall.

A tall man appeared in the doorway, a cowboy hat on his head, a shiny badge on his beige shirt, Pearl Lawrence at his side. He gripped her upper arm. "Afternoon, folks." Deputy Hicks peered around his shoulder.

Mr. Bell squeezed in. "Sheriff Ryan here found Miss Lawrence on the other side of the bridge."

"Escaping," the sheriff said.

"I'm not going to be blamed," she declared. High color stained her cheeks. Her smart dress had not fared well on her journey. "Mr. Rogers, you tell them. I didn't have nothing to do with Ray's death."

"I believe you," the club owner said, "but you shouldn't have run." His gaze slewed to McElroy. "Not smart to run when you're up against the law. It's like an admission of guilt."

"But I couldn't stay and——."

"Rogers," the sheriff interrupted. "Al Rogers? Galveston?"

His relaxed pose didn't change, but the diamond flashed as if he'd jerked. "That's me. What can I do for you, Sheriff?"

"I hear the dead man came here with you, on Wednesday."

"Careful, Sheriff. Ray Anderson's sister is here, Miss Cat Anderson."

He gestured toward her. "And we're having an interesting conversation you should listen to. Are you acquainted with Hank McElroy, Boone Galvin, and Paul Jackson?"

"Jackson I've met. Sir. And Mr. McElroy." He nodded toward the older man.

"McElroy Senior is no longer as important as his son." Hicks snorted at Rogers' wry comment. The club owner paused then continued smoothly. "That shift in status may have something to do with his behavior. May I introduce Hank McElroy and his new bride? And there on the end, beside Rev. Thomas, that's Boone Galvin. These three men are the owners of Texas P & R. Anderson, the man who died, he was running a game to get shares in their company."

"On your orders, Rogers?"

The man's eyes narrowed. The fire blazed. Nedda shivered at the sharp gaze. Then Rogers tempered his anger. Mr. Phillips eased back into his seat, no longer on alert.

"You'll find no evidence linking me to Anderson's plan."

"But he owed you a lot of money."

"A few of my clubs, yes. That money's lost to me now." He shrugged. "Bad debt. As I said, we're having an interesting conversation. Mrs. McElroy here—she's the bride, Sheriff. Offer your congratulations to the groom." He paused until the sheriff acknowledged Nedda then resumed. "Mrs. McElroy had just determined that we had no reason to want Mr. Anderson dead. Alive, I would recover my losses. Isn't that right, McElroy?" He turned to the older man.

"That's right," he begrudged.

"Your deputy would have reached the same conclusion, weeks from now."

"*You're* doing my job, Rogers?"

"Not me." He gestured to Nedda. "Mrs. McElroy's turning the pieces over and slotting them into place."

Nedda's cheeks heated.

"I think we should continue to let her lead," Rev. Thomas said gently. "She shows a clear rationale."

"A woman at the job?" Sheriff Ryan's doubt raised his eyebrows. "Let's hear what you have to say, ma'am, before we judge anything. Here, Pearlie, take a seat," and he gave her a little push into the room.

Mr. Phillips stood to offer his chair, and the woman sank into it. Mud caked her pumps. Her stockings were laddered, and blood streaked her ankles. Her simple dress was mud-splashed, still damp around the hem, with little rips in the skirt. The boxer eased her into his chair then perched on the open windowsill, arms folded across his chest.

Nedda found it hard to meet Mr. Phillips' flat stare. "According to Mr. Stringer, you left the study last night, during the storm. You climbed through the window and used the back porch stairs."

"Weasel," he judged without heat. Mr. Stringer scooted his chair inches away. "What of it? I went to Pearl's room."

"We're in love," she cried dramatically.

That claim confused Nedda. "I thought you came with Ray."

"That was for show. Ray wanted it that way. He said he had to have a date for this wedding."

"Leave her be," Phillips growled. "She didn't do nothing."

"She fled the scene of a murder," Sheriff Ryan insisted.

"Yep, she's stupid, but she's my stupid. She didn't kill Anderson. I didn't kill him either."

"No," Nedda agreed, "I didn't think you killed him." She took a deep reassuring breath. The next was a wild guess, but the clues were there. They just had to be pointed out. "And with you gone from the parlor, Mr. Phillips, that means Mr. Stringer has no alibi for his whereabouts during the storm."

It took the room a whole second before they caught what she'd said. Mr. Stringer started up. "What? You think I killed Anderson?"

"For a man who works in Houston," she said calmly, laying out her evidence, "you know quite a lot about the seedier side of Galveston. You know Mr. Rogers here and Mr. Phillips. Mr. Rogers wanted Ray alive. Mr. Phillips follows Mr. Rogers' orders. Ray collected secrets to use as blackmail. What secrets of yours had Ray collected, Mr. Stringer? How long had he been blackmailing you?"

He dove for the window. His chair crashed onto the floor.

Phillips grabbed his shirt. The fabric ripped but held. He hauled Stringer back into the room, gave him a brain-tumbling shake, then dumped him to the floor.

"Your murderer, Sheriff Ryan," Rogers said then added, "I need a whiskey."

Nedda pressed a hand to her beating heart.

. ~ . ~ . ~ .

"How did you know?" Sheriff Ryan asked her later.

Deputy Hicks had left, hauling the handcuffed Stringer to the county jail and the shrouded Anderson to the county morgue.

"You heard what I asked him."

"That's little enough to go on." He thumbed through the black notebook that Deputy Hicks had found in his search of Ray's room. The pages detailed payments from over ten sources, people referenced only by their initials. They had paid and paid to keep their secrets hidden.

Hank's arm rested heavy on her shoulders, but Nedda welcomed the grounding weight. She still couldn't believe that her guess had been true.

"I did have an advantage over you, Sheriff. Law enforcement looks on everyone with suspicion, don't you? I *knew* the people who could not be potential murderers. Hank and Colfax, Paul, Boone, they're not murderers. Rev. Thomas didn't have the hand strength. Mr. Culpepper had no connection to Ray, and Ray never gave him a glance. He did look at Mr. Stringer. He had an odd smile when he looked at him. Once Mr. McElroy and Mr. Rogers lost any motive to kill Ray, then the murder had to be a personal reason, not a financial conspiracy."

"How did you decide on Stringer? I'll have to explain it to the district attorney when he gets back from New Orleans. You can't tell me that you decided on the man based on one look."

"No, I didn't really remember that, not until Deputy Hicks put handcuffs on him. But it had to be someone familiar with Houston and Galveston. Mr. Stringer is a reporter in Houston, and he covers the oil industry news. Last night he regaled me with stories about clubs and other places in Galveston. The kind of places that Ray frequented."

"That's slim evidence."

"Strong enough evidence when it's lacking in everyone else." She'd learned that from her former employer, making decisions based on one trickle of information, a vital piece because everything else pointed in a different direction. *Here,* Mr. Ingram had told her more than once when a connection paid off, *pay attention to the little details. They add up to millions.* She missed Mr. Ingram.

"McElroy Senior, he's got connections in Houston and Galveston."

"True, but Ray served him better alive than dead. He was probably milking Ray of his blackmail money. He may know who those initials are, Sheriff. You should ask him."

"And so he may." He clapped his hands to his knees and stood. "Well, I'll be making my way back to town. You'll need to stop by the jail on Monday, to make an official statement, all of you."

"Will there be a trial?" Cat asked, subdued.

"Not if Stringer pleads to the charge of murder."

"May I visit him?"

"You're the sister? You *want* to talk to him? Well, I'll not stop you. Tell him that the judge will look on him with favor if he accepts a plea bargain."

"I'll tell him that, sheriff."

. ~ . ~ . ~ .

They lingered two more weeks at the Back Bay Inn. After Monday at the Sheriff's office, Hank threw himself into the physical labor of storm clean-up with the Bells. Nedda drove Cat daily to visit.

Ray was buried at week's end at a moss-draped cemetery in Baytown. Cat was dry-eyed throughout and refused to talk, but she wept in her room after, alone.

Nedda rang Boone, but problems in Houston delayed his return. He came at the weekend, though, and Cat was to ride back with him.

Colfax would travel from Houston to the Sacred Heart Academy in northern Louisiana. He hitched a ride with Boone to catch the train to his school.

As they prepared to leave, Boone letting the engine idle to warm it before the long drive, Nedda leaned through the back car window and ruffled Colfax's hair, lightened by the Texas sun. "I think you've added inches over the summer. Your father won't recognize you."

He chuckled. "I won't recognize *him*! You think he'll let me finish next year at the Academy? I'd like to graduate with my friends."

"And so you will," she vowed firmly. "If it comes to it, I'll argue the point with Sheridan. And win. I still hold his proxy, you know." She straightened and tapped the auto's door. "Cat, he'll require a day of shopping. Stop groaning, Colfax. You need clothes and new shoes."

"I have plenty."

"You've outgrown your shirts and your pants. And that boot has a hole in the sole. A full day, Cat."

"I'll see he has what he needs, never you fret." Her gaze drifted over the lawn, greened by the soaking rains of the storm. Beyond the green, the waves rolled, the current still strong as creeks flooded in with the remnant of the hurricane's rain. A regal heron flew across the waters. "This place *is* beautiful. I wish——."

"There are other beautiful places."

She blinked. "Yes, there are. We'll find them."

As the touring car turned between the pines, sparser now that the deadfall had been hauled away, Cat laughed at something Boone said, and Nedda's heart lightened. She waved one last time then turned to Hank, leaning against him as the touring car vanished behind the pines.

"And now, Mr. McElroy?"

"And now, Mrs. McElroy, rest, relaxation, and the Texas hill country. I've a friend has a house on a lake. You will love it."

"That's what these two weeks were *supposed* to be. Rest. Relaxation. A tranquil wedding."

His blue eyes glinted. "Well, we managed the wedding. Second time be charm for the relaxation and tranquility."

"As long as we don't require a third attempt."

Hank laughed and kissed her.

.~.~.~.~.~.

Thank You!

Thank you for reading a story in the new **Courting Trouble** series. I hope you've enjoyed our time with Nedda Courtland.

The trilogy **Courting Trouble** is a side series to the main **Into Death** series. The first novel in that series, *Digging into Death*, was my first completed manuscript—but I held off on publishing it, one of my few wise moves.

After I published the first three Regency mysteries in the **Hearts in Hazard** series, I picked up *Digging into Death*, doubled the number of suspects, reworked several ideas, and published it in 2016.

Because of her early advent in my writing, **Into Death's** main character Isabella remains attached to my soul, and now her friend Nedda Courtland adds a second layer of attachment.

When I published *Sailing with Mystery* in 2023, I waved goodbye to Isabella and looked forward to writing novels with Flick Sherbourne, the second protagonist in *Portrait with Death*. Those stories are still on the horizon, yet here I am with stories for Nedda that surprised me when they jumped into my mind.

This collection is three novelettes ~ *Spanish Moss, Texas Sun,* and *Gulf Storm.*

. ~ . ~ . ~ .

For any questions, comments, and speculations, please contact winkbooks@aol.com. Information and links are on the website Writers Ink Books. Look for M.'s titles at online distributors both nationally and internationally.

Please subscribe to M.'s seasonal newsletter for up-to-date information about her fiction and nonfiction as well as recent releases. Contact either winkbooks@aol.com or use the following link to join the newsletter AND receive a free mystery short story >> "The Lion's Den" https://dl.bookfunnel.com/wc84divkre

Please write a review.

Indie writers thrive on freely-given reviews. We're small beans here; we don't have the advertising budget of the Big Peeps. Of course, with *any* book that you enjoy, please share with other readers looking for escape from the dark stresses of life. That's the reason we write.

More Fiction from M.A. Lee

Into Death, a series set in the 1920s

Digging into Death ~ A governess seeking refuge, a handsome young man, an archaeological dig on the island of Crete. Romance is inevitable; murder is not. Suspicions escalate, artifacts are stolen, and then a second murder. Has the love of her life beguiled Isabella straight into death? Available in paperback and e-book

Christmas with Death ~ Christmas is for miracles, merriment, and murder. Set in 1919 at an English country manor for a party throughout Christmastide. Available in paperback and e-book.

Portrait with Death ~ Isabella and her new friend Flick stumble upon the body of George Webberly, a teacher at Greavley Abbey School. Why would anyone kill a school master? Motives abound, and suspects increase. Who committed the murder? Can Isabella find the answer?

These three titles are in the anthology **Into Death**. https://books2read.com/u/baDN1L

Sailing into Mystery ~ Mystery and peril are dangerous shipmates for an ocean voyage.

Isabella travels to rejoin her husband Madoc, currently in India, and encounters puzzles and intrigue.

The collection includes a stolen diary in "Amber Dreams", poison pen letters in "Purple Poison", mischievous pranks in "Black Heart", jewelry theft in "Silver Web", and lethal spies in "The Red Mask".

The collection can be found at this link: https://books2read.com/u/3R5QJR

Courting Trouble ~ Three invitations from death.

"Spanish Moss" finds Nedda Courtland in New Orleans where she encounters love and poison.

For the novelette "Texas Sun", sabotage and an attempted murder occur at an oil patch.

In "Gulf Storm", a hurricane wreaks destruction while evil causes murder.

"Spanish Moss" can be found at this link:

https://books2read.com/u/bPM11l

"Texas Sun" can be found at this link: https://books2read.com/u/4XM6k6

Hearts in Hazard
12 novels of Regency Mystery with a Dash of Romance

1 ~ *A Game of Secrets* ~ Smugglers, secrets and spies: Kate tries to hide in plain sight; Tony tries to catch a spy. First they fall in love, then they fall into trouble with smugglers. Will they survive?

The book that began M.A. Lee's writing career. https://books2read.com/u/bPKoZz

2 ~ *A Game of Spies* ~ Salons and soirées, flirtation and dancing, gambling and spies: Josette and Giles fall in love over a deck of cards—and try not to die.

Spymaster Giles Hargreaves was introduced in *A Game of Secrets*.

3 ~ *A Game of Hearts* ~ Two couples :: One titled widow, one wealthy businessman: two hearts shadowed by their past. One bright young flirt, one hard-edged young man: two hearts crossed by circumstance. Mix in a courtesan and two rakes, all out for mischief, and murder bloody and foul.

A Trio of Games ~ a collection of these three novels. https://books2read.com/u/boqEJp

4 ~ *The Danger of Secrets* ~ Deep in the wintry countryside, a house warmed by relatives and friends: secrets of family, secrets of hearts, secrets of blood and pain. Match a daughter to an unknown father; match a spinster to an earl; match a serial killer to his next victim.

Gordon Musgrove was introduced in *A Game of Spies*.

5 ~ *The Danger for Spies* ~ Impossibilities? Rakes don't lose their hearts. Spies don't give up the game. No one hides in plain sight. Codes are unbreakable. A man can't hold onto revenge for years and years. Impossibilities are designed to be shattered.

Toby Kennitt was introduced in *A Game of Spies*.

6 ~ *The Danger to Hearts* ~ A country manor in early Spring: older woman and younger man. Horses, cats, needlework, roses and afternoon teas ~ What could possibly go wrong in an idyll? Trouble in the past, trouble now, and murder.

The character Jess Carter was introduced in *A Game of Secrets*.

A Trio of Dangers ~ the 2nd three Hearts in Hazard collection. https://books2read.com/u/mVDxP5

7 ~ *The Key to Secrets* ~ Debutantes should snare fiancés, not

murder them. Constable Hector Evans must solve three murders. Is his former love guilty, or is she a convenient scapegoat?

Constable Hector Evans was introduced in *The Danger to Hearts*.

8 ~ *The Key for Spies* ~ Spies and traitors. Lies and treachery. Unexpected love where bullets fly. One traitor destroys loyalty. What will two traitors destroy?

9 ~ *The Key with Hearts* ~ A convenient marriage inconveniently causes murder.

A Trio of Keys ~ the 3rd three Hearts in Hazard collection. https://books2read.com/u/bPe6wY

10 ~ *The Hazard of Secrets* .~ Two hearts with dangerous pasts— Can they keep their secrets, or will murder force them to reveal all?

11 ~ *The Hazard for Spies* ~ Disguised to spy. Will murder destroy their chance for love?

12 ~ *The Hazard with Hearts* ~ Two wives haunt the castle. Will she be the third to die?

A Trio of Hazards ~ the 4th three Hearts in Hazard collection. https://books2read.com/u/4jNBkY

Miss Beale Writes
A Touch of Gothic, A Touch of Mystery, A Touch of Romance

1 ~ *The Dark Lord* ~ Everyone knows there's no such thing as ghosts. Tell that to the two ghosts haunting Elizabeth.

A mystery novella of Regency England. https://books2read.com/u/38yprZ

2 ~ *The Bride in Ghostly White* ~ Unfortunate accident? Or premeditated death? Only the ghost knows, and she's not telling.

A mystery novella of Victorian England. COMING SOON!

Perils in Lace and Hard Iron ~ the duo novellas collected together. COMING SOON!

Wild Sherwood series
Historical Legend fused with the Faeries of British Myth ~ A Collaboration of Edie Roones & M. A Lee

Into Wild Sherwood ~ an anthology of five short stories
"Tod the Fox and the Faeries in the Ring" :: *Never enter a Faerie Ring. The Faeries like to play.*
With the guards of Nottingham on his heels, Tod flees to wild Sherwood Forest. Frightened in the night, he falls into a Faerie Ring. Faeries play with their catch, whether in the Ring or on the Wild Hunt. How can he escape them?
"The Poisoner and the Faerie Huntsman" :: *Never reveal weakness to a Faerie.*
Escaping a false accusation of poisoning, Melly and her hound hide from pursuit in Sherwood Forest. That night, she encounters the black hounds of the Wild Hunt. Then the Huntsman arrives. Has she fallen into greater trouble?
"Three Yule Feasts for Faeries" :: *Will the cook become the final dish?*
Yule: the worst time of year for Ellen Best. Then a Faerie knocks at her door. Two dinners, he proposes, and a final feast for his duchess. After each, she'll receive payment. Yet what did the Faerie mean by *final* feast?
"Friar Tuck and the Faerie at the Pool" :: *No one escapes from Faeries.*
Friar Tuck encounters a Faerie at a cool forest pool. She is wondrous and strange and deadly. How can he convince her that he is a man of peace, unlike the guards and rangers who hunt in the forest?
"Alan-a-Dale and the Harp of Elandrielle" :: *Who can trust a Faerie?*
The song competition at Nottingham's Winter Feast offers a purse that will pay Alan-a-Dale's debts. He wins the first night's round … offending his competitors who take revenge. At his lowest point, a Faerie finds him. She offers him a bargain—yet who can trust a Faerie?
Link to this anthology: https://books2read.com/u/bOzoDE

Outlaws of Wild Sherwood ~ the second anthology with five short stories
"A Twist of Faerie Magic" :: *A twist of murder. A twist of Faerie magic. And Dav the wrestler caught between.*
When Dav is accused of murdering his true love's husband, will magic reveal the true culprit?
"A Faerie Song for a Feast" :: *Masks, Mummers, and a Faerie Song*
Alan-a-Dale risks playing a song learned in the land of Faeries to help Robin Hood and his men. Will the song help or hinder the outlaws?
"Mischief of a Faerie" :: *A Challenge with Quarterstaves*
When his sister names a bearded giant as her newborn's father, Arthur

storms off to force Little John to support them. Yet how can a simple poacher defeat a man taller and stronger than he is?

"The Green Man" :: *A Venture with Destiny*

Bad luck has plagued Jack Greenleaf for years. Abandoned, evicted, and rejected, he joined the other outcasts in Sherwood Forest. The Green Man of the Faerie may seal his fate.

"The Prize of a Golden Arrow" :: *By Hook or Crook or Arrow*

Gil vowed never again to take up the long bow. Then he learns the May Day archery contest is a trap to capture Robin Hood. He resolves to foil the Sheriff's plan.

Link to this anthology: https://books2read.com/u/4Aj99N

Out of Wild Sherwood ~ the third anthology with five short stories

"Dangerous Gold" :: *Strong Temptation for Two Young Thieves*

Haunted by misgivings, Dav of Doncaster keeps a wary eye on two young thieves … only to discover a lethal trap is closing fast.

"Keen-Edged Dagger" :: *Murder needs a Tricky Vengeance*

Falsely accused of murder, Brigit scrambles to prove her innocence … or to get the justice her cousin deserves.

"Silver Dreams" :: *A Double Twist for a Double Theft*

Quick and fleet, Finn Callum is guilty of much but never a blood crime. To wake with a knife aimed between his eyes is a shock.

"Poisoned Roots" :: *A Deadly Sin caused Dishonor*

Outcast from his family, Much aches to restore his good name and honor. Then he hears of trouble at his old home. Will death cauterize that old wound?

"Memory of Magic" :: *A Faerie Confronts Human Evil*

The hunter Fenric stumbles upon slaughtered deer, killed for neither food nor sport. The trail leads the Faerie beyond Sherwood and to a freehold stinking of evil.

Link to this anthology: https://books2read.com/u/mlQvM7

. ~ . ~ . ~ .

Edie Roones also writes novellas in the **Wild Sherwood** series. The first one, *The Hooded Outlaw*, features Robin Hood and Lady Marianne. Additional novellas with Will Scarlet, Much the Miller's Son, and Little John will follow.

All books from Writers' Ink are available at online distributors everywhere.

Visit www.writersinkbooks.com

for Quick Links under the author pages for M.A. Lee and Edie Roones.

For any comments, questions, and speculations, contact winkbooks@aol.com. Use the subject line to aim your email to a specific book or series or author.

Excerpts from M.A. Lee's Fiction

Opening Chapters from four Works by M.A. Lee

Digging into Death ~ from Chapter 1

From the first novel of the **Into Death** series *Digging into Death*, featuring Isabella Newcombe:

> *Budding artist Isabella Newcombe finds herself stranded at an archaeological dig. Madoc Tarrant convinces his brother Prof. Gawen Tarrant to hire Isabella as the dig's illustrator.*
> *Romance is inevitable. Murder is not.*

If ever a maiden needed a hero, Isabella did.

Crete was the famed birthplace of Zeus, the god who granted supplicants' prayers. Standing on the steps of the Heraklion Hotel, Isabella hoped her hero appeared before a blood sacrifice was necessary.

She plunked down her suitcase on the hotel steps and fanned her wide-brimmed straw hat. In ancient Crete the rulers had offered shelter and protection to strangers. Yet in the closed faces of the passers-by, intent on their errands, she did not see any hospitality offered to a foreign woman alone. She needed a recognizable and friendly face. She didn't see one.

Men talking, engines sputtering, horns blaring, dogs barking, donkeys braying: after the hotel's quiet, the cacophony assaulted her ears. Men poured past the steps with scarcely a glance at her. Most wore the dark Cretan jacket and loose breeches, although a few suits testified to modern Europe's inroads on island culture. A few women in unrelieved black walked along the dusty road, but they ignored the lone foreigner on the hotel steps.

Isabella saw no one familiar and definitely no one who looked like the reincarnation of a protective god and certainly no one who could rescue a stranded governess.

Then a demigod emerged from the hotel. Like Apollo, god of light and knowledge, his golden hair glinted in the morning light. And Isabella recognized him: Nigel Arkwright, one of the English archaeologists.

Prof. Arkwright had dined with her erstwhile employer on Tuesday night. Last night, in the bar, she'd seen him order one whiskey after another. This morning, though, her panic when the hotel manager confronted her about her bill had cast him from her mind. But he could give her help. Although Isabella despised encroachers, she couldn't let this god-given opportunity slip away.

As he reached the last step, she dropped her heavy suitcase in his path. "Prof. Arkwright, hello. I'm Isabella Newcombe. We met when the Harcourt-Smythes visited your dig last weekend."

His mouth compressed, which didn't bode well for her start. Last evening's drinking might have been too deep for an appeal to his English gentleman's code. A hangover this morning wouldn't help her.

He cleared his throat. "I remember you. You were the governess." He looked past her, scanning the road. "American governess, wasn't it?"

"Yes, I *was* the governess." She stressed the past tense. She hitched her satchel strap higher on her shoulder. "They discharged me."

"I'm sorry to hear that, Miss, but I'm in a—."

"No, you're not sorry. You do not care. You don't know me well enough to care. You don't know me at all. And that is the crux of my problem, Prof. Arkwright. Besides my former employers, no one knows me here, and no one cares. I am in a foreign country, surrounded by foreigners, and I do not have enough money for my passage home."

"Your appeal should go to your employer, not to me."

"No matter what circumstance, I will not return to him." She hoped the bright glare hid her flaming cheeks. "Two weeks' wages and a letter for his bank in Athens were all that Mr. Harcourt-Smythe gave me. I can repay you once I reach Athens. I do have the funds. My problem is here and now."

"Surely someone—."

"I am completely alone, and I might as well be penniless. Then I saw you. I thought Providence had sent you to be my rescuer."

"Miss Newcombe," he settled a pith helmet on his gilded hair, "I don't believe I qualify as a rescuer." The narrow brim shaded his eyes.

She hated this intruding role she'd been thrust into, but she played it with the desperate energy that stressed its truth. "Here am I, stranded and virtually penniless. Here are you, an English gentleman in the midst of an important dig. You must have need of a helper. Someone who can catalog items or type notes or—or do something. Surely an extra pair of hands can be useful somewhere."

A horn honked. Prof. Arkwright looked around. An army truck jolted along the street. He glanced back at her as he stepped down to meet it. "Miss Newcombe, I'm not in charge of this dig. Gawen Tarrant is. I have no power to hire anyone. And he has no liking for tourists who need their hands held."

"Professor, I am desperate. I will do anything. Please, say you'll help me. Please don't abandon me."

The truck jerked to a stop and bounced when the driver pulled the brake. Leaving the motor running, he jumped out. The professor started to the front of the truck.

"Prof. Arkwright?" Isabella pleaded.

He looked back at her as he dropped a *baksheesh* into the young man's hand. Then he dug into his pocket for another coin. "Ari, shove Miss Newcombe's case into the back."

Isabella nearly sank with relief, but Prof. Arkwright had already reached the driver's door. Ari lifted her heavy suitcase and swung it into the back. The professor revved the motor impatiently, and she clambered gracelessly into the passenger seat. He released the parking brake. The truck jolted off. She looked back.

Ari stood waving on the bottom step. Behind him, the Heraklion Hotel loomed, substantial but unwelcoming to a single, penniless woman.

She wasn't sure which appeal to the gentleman's chivalric code had changed Prof. Arkwright's mind, and she wouldn't ask. As the truck jounced over furrows and eroded ruts, she worried about her unsecured suitcase bouncing in the back, but she didn't ask about that either. The roar of the engine hid the grumbles from her days-empty stomach.

Close to Heraklion they had smooth driving, yet a few miles outside the capitol the road had fallen into disrepair, a casualty of the recent war. It became disreputable as they rolled the miles around the north of Mount Dikte.

As he drove, Nigel Arkwright's jaw jutted pugnaciously. When they left the main road, the way disintegrated into a cart track winding through the eastern foothills of the mountain that guides still claimed had been the birthplace of Zeus. Snow already frosted its heights.

The professor ground the gears as they halted for herds of sheep and workers repairing an eroded irrigation ditch and children playing in the tiny hamlets. The roosters and chickens scattered ahead of the truck. Not once did he speak to her.

Isabella clamped her jaw to keep from biting her tongue. She wanted to ask about the passing landscape or about the dig at Knossos and why Arkwright's group wasn't working the famous site. A look at his undimmed frown daunted her.

From the visit last weekend, she knew that Arkwright and his colleagues worked two obscure sites far from the four better-known digs of Knossos, Phaestos, Mallia, and Gurnia. Compared to those, this expedition could hardly carry an official name. Only Zeus' own mountain gave grace to the sites.

Isabella and the Harcourt-Smythes had arrived at the dig after a pouring rain had collapsed a wall. Muck the flat color of cement had covered everything and everyone. The artist lurking inside Isabella had taken the mud and exposed foundations and imagined a country palace, braced against the bleaching sun and African winds. Her two charges had distracted her from that past. The busy archaeologists had barely acknowledged their unexpected visitors.

As Prof. Arkwright man-handled the truck over the road, Isabella stared at the craggy rocks of Mt. Dikte, scarred with ravines and pocked with tumbled boulders. These English archaeologists might not be the answer to her prayer. Should she have looked for a different rescuer? Should she have waited? She remembered two married ladies at the dig but no single ones. The dig would still be busy, and she was an imposition. Would they welcome her at all? Would they give her a chance to earn her passage to England? Or had she only delayed the inevitable?

Last night she had wanted to scream with fear and frustration. Instead, she paced through the early hours as she tried to work out a solution to her unexpected unemployment.

This late in the year, few archaeologists remained on Crete. She had planned to search each group out; if they had failed her, she would approach the English construction crew working on the roads or haunt the antiquities museum. Yet a search took money, and she needed to hoard the pittance that was her only protection against the world until she reached Athens. And that was before the hotel manager demanded she pay from Tuesday through Friday.

Nigel Arkwright had seemed a gift from the gods. If he weren't, she had still gained time to contrive a less desperate solution.

The god Apollo was steering his sun chariot to its westward descent when they arrived at the dig. Arkwright jolted his mundane chariot to a stop. The professor set the hand brake but left the motor running. As she reached for the door handle, he said, "At least you can be silent. After this morning's deluge, I wasn't certain."

"I was desperate, Professor. If I had not convinced you, I don't know what I would have done. The hotel manager had decided I was a disreputable nuisance once he learned that Mr. Harcourt-Smythe had discharged me. I must thank you once again, Prof. Arkwright."

"I haven't helped yet. That's not in my power. As I said, I'm not in charge here."

"Yes, you mentioned Professor Tarrant. He wasn't here last weekend."

"Gawen Tarrant was at Knossos on a shared week, our fourth this season. You may have seen his brother, although he tried to avoid your party. Tourists are a nuisance who interrupt our work. Your arrival will interrupt us again."

She sucked in a breath. "Thank you for the warning."

"Our work requires training and education, Miss Newcombe, so you will not waltz into a position. My wife sorts and catalogs the daily finds at the palace site. Prof. Standings is in charge of the temple site; his wife assists him there. Tarrant handles his own notes, as do I. I don't know what Standings does. The students will not need a secretary. Unless you can contrive a job before you meet Tarrant, you will soon return to Heraklion. All the chatter in the world won't change his mind. Indeed, you will find it decides him more quickly. That, too, is a warning."

Speech delivered, he shoved open the truck door and strode away, shouting to a worker to drive it up to the house.

Find *Digging into Death* **here**: https://books2read.com/u/bzdM72

Trailer   https://www.youtube.com/watch?v=zX1BPx6VUnU

The Hazard for Spies ~ from Chapter 1

From a Regency mystery novel, part of the **Hearts in Hazard** series *The Hazard for Spies*, each novel featuring a different couple. These twelve novels are stand-alones.

When Phinney Darracott's sister and brother-in-law died, their children whispered "murder". Several mysterious circumstances occur before Phinney believes them.

Seeking justice for their murders, she follows the clues to London. The lawyer at the center of the tangle of clues is shot dead while she watches from a hiding place.

Will she discover the connection between past and present murders?

Phinney tucked a dark tress back under the ruffled mobcap that topped her disguise as a cleaning maid.

Light glowed down the hall in a side office. While no one was present, someone obviously worked late. A clerk from the ground floor, she had guessed as she picked up crumbled paper that had missed the dustbin. She smoothed out the documents that had a clerk working into the small hours then folded them and tucked them into a pocket for later perusal.

The other offices needed only a cursory cleaning. She used the master key given her by Mr. Gregory to re-lock each office as she finished. "Never can be too careful, not with lawyers and their documents," the older man had said, his esses whistling through a missing tooth. "You keep everything locked good and tight, Mrs. Coates."

Phinney had nodded and accepted the key with a solemn promise to keep it on her person.

She didn't grin at this unexpected luck until Mr. Gregory headed off to deal with a creaking shutter.

Her luck continued to hold. She had only the two top floors to clean while Mrs. Gregory took the bottom two. Mr. Gregory fixed problems, did the heavy work, and maintained the cellars with its large coal bin.

As she slipped into the offices of *Titterstone & Montjoy, Solicitors*, she gave a fleeting thought to the children, sleeping soundly at the mission. She had tucked up Hank then reminded Elise to put aside her reading before the downstairs clock struck the eighth hour. Bright blue eyes sparkling with mischief, her niece complained but acquiesced. Vic had a primer and pencil, working on the alphabet that Elise was trying to teach him.

Vic might not be family, but he formed part of their little family now, the three children and her, alone against the world.

Vic had warned them to flee from Liverpool. After trouble with press gangs, Phinney hadn't hesitated to hustle them onto the first coach out of the city. The boy had then protected their journey to Parton March. Once they were settled, seemingly safe, Phinney had tried to leave the children at the estate. She hadn't reached the neighboring village before she demanded the carter return her to the house. She couldn't leave them with strangers, even if the strangers seemed trustworthy.

Now she stood in the offices of *Titterstone & Montjoy*, convinced the two upstanding attorneys were criminals.

She had lucked into the job as cleaner. Mr. Gregory accepted her disguise as a war widow desperate to support her three children.

At Parton March, she had avoided any interaction with the two lawyers, there to serve their wealthy client as he determined his heirs. Even with murder and attempted murder, she kept herself and the children closeted, well away from the family and guests. She knew of George Titterstone and Kennedy Montjoy from Rosie's correspondence. Her sister poured out in a letter that Peter's father had involved himself in another *contretemps* on a business venture. In resolving the issue, the son had fallen out with his father and severed the connection when they left London.

Phinney only vaguely remembered those months before her sister and brother-in-law were killed. Working as a governess of four children had consumed all her energies. She barely had a half-hour each day to herself. Her meals were taken with the children. Her employer required daily reports of the children's progress and weekly proof of that progress. The older girl was a dreamer; the twin boys were pranksters who preferred fishing and roaming to Latin and ciphers, and the youngest girl would sneak to the kitchen for a sweet from the cook. She had tucked Rosie's letter in her reticule and forgotten it—until she drew it out at the Lintons.

She shook herself mentally. Brown studies were an indulgence. She had offices to search.

A whisk over the surfaces with her duster, then she carried her lamp into Mr. Titterstone's inner office. Last night she had searched Mr. Montjoy's office. She wanted one document with Peter's name or even his father's, Pierre DeChambeaux. One document, to prove she was on the right track.

The kneehole desk had six drawers, three on each side. Mr. Titterstone had double-framed windows at his back. His partner had only one window and the smaller of the two offices. Mr. Montjoy's window view, however, looked toward the park at the end of the block. On a fine day he would see treetops and catch glimpses of flowers. Mr. Titterstone overlooked the street and the red-bricked building across the way, yet he had an inner closet with a narrow bed, washbasin, and shelving for boxed documents.

George Titterstone also worked more cases than his partner. A dozen labelled boxes were stacked on shelves to one side of the room. Phinney eyed those case files and wondered how long a perusal of each would take. She might need several nights to work through all of the files.

Tucking her cleaning basket with rags and wax polish beside the shelves, she approached the desk, choosing Mr. Titterstone's side. She quickly scanned the stacked ledgers and the documents inside folders, careful not to disarrange them. Her father hadn't liked any of his papers moved, especially when he prepared a sermon. Phinney had picked up items, dusted underneath, then replaced them, all without the Rev. Darracott spotting the removals. Finding nothing, she tugged on the center drawer. It didn't budge. Slipping fingers under her mobcap, she withdrew two hair picks and set to work on the simple lock, mentally thanking Vic for his lessons.

When the clock in the outer office chimed the half-hour, Phinney climbed from her aching knees and glared at the desk. Nothing. Not a single paper with the name *DeChambeaux*. Only a couple of files had dates preceding the carriage accident, but those were innocuous statements about an estate called Ridings in Little Houghton, inherited by Sir Charles Audley from his uncle. Mr. Titterstone had jotted a half-page of notes about the classics scholar who was decoding Egyptian hieroglyphs from the Rosetta Stone. Three words in a different hand appended the note: *Poutaine, cipher, key.*

She slipped the note back into the file box, telling herself the intervening years would have resolved any issue. Yet those three words niggled at her as she searched the other drawers. Hands on her hips, she considered retrieving it, yet even as she reached for the drawer, the door to the outer office opened. Hurriedly, she grabbed up a cleaning cloth.

When Titterstone's office door opened, Phinney stayed crouched beside her basket and pretended to dust the bottom shelf.

"Here. Who are you?"

She straightened. Without looking in the man's direction, she bobbed a curtsey. "The cleaner, sir."

"I hadn't—you are here alone."

Phinney stiffened. "The Gregorys are below, sir," she snipped. "This floor is my duty. And the one below."

"It can't be."

At the confusing comment, Phinney chanced a look to see a tall, broad-shouldered man, black hair and pale skin, blue eyes so pale they looked like tinted glass. Her mouth dropped open.

Conrad Hoppock laughed. "It *is* you."

Find *The Hazard for Spies* **here:** https://books2read.com/u/4j2JEl
Trailer https://youtu.be/YrnFtNhzwQs

The Dark Lord ~ from Chapter 1

From *The Dark Lord,* a standalone gothic mystery novella.
*When Elizabeth Fortescue comes to Feldstone Grange, she expects Baron
Harcourt to turn her away as too young and too pretty. Yet the baron is desperate to
hire someone; the former housekeepers all abandoned their positions.
Elizabeth soon discovers the reason.
Everyone knows there's no such thing as ghosts.
Tell that to the two ghosts haunting Elizabeth.*

"You're not to look at 'im."

That order about meeting her future employer certainly surprised
Elizabeth. "I beg your pardon?"

The whiskered withered man did not himself look at her. He hadn't
stopped or even hesitated as he led her along the back hall. The dark
paneled walls absorbed the light from the few sconces. On a sunny day,
windows would admit the radiant sun and warm the shadowed interior.
On this rainy day, the wind created a chilling numbness, and gloom
dominated, oppressive and unwelcoming.

"He don't like being gawked at," the older man said. "You keep your
head down, eyes on the floor." He muttered something else.

"My apologies," Elizabeth was forced to say, not daring to let
anything slip in her quest for a new position. She'd traveled up from
London, jounced along in badly sprung coaches, squeezed between smelly
passengers, her savings eking away at every overnight stop. The service
agency hadn't guaranteed a position. Apparently, Baron Harcourt wished
to interview any potential employee. "I did not hear what you said, good
sir."

"I said 'It'll be lucky if'n you last the first week'."

"I am stronger than I appear."

"Aye, well, that's to be seen. The others didn't last."

"Do all servants follow that rule, sir?"

"The ones that want to keep their positions."

That certainly depressed her. Keeping her eyes down constantly—she
didn't know if that were possible. She'd never followed such a rule.
Indeed, her father had always warned her and her mother to keep their
eyes up and open, watching fellow wayfarers for potential trouble, spying
the land for potential *ambuscadoes.* Following the drum had entailed
heightened caution, and since she'd entered service five years ago, she

found that the wiser course.

A housekeeper would be expected to assume her responsibilities quickly. "What is the number of staff?"

"His lordship will tell you." The man stopped before a door with matched panels, triple circles carved inside each square. He didn't knock, just opened the door and stepped back. "His lordship will be up from the stables momentarily. Stand before his desk. Don't touch nothing!"

He'd shut the door before she gained the rug.

Eyes down, she shivered. Rain had seeped through the dove-grey redingote she wore like a uniform. The fire behind smoked a little, but the heat didn't penetrate her wet clothes. She dreaded to think what her hair looked like. She could feel tendrils plastered to her neck and her cheeks. The old man had taken her boiled wool cloak and her soaked hat, its shape lost to the steady rain. Without the cloak, she had immediately chilled.

A half-hour passed, tolled by the great clock in the entrance hall. The fire's heat started to penetrate her clothing. Elizabeth no longer shivered incessantly. And she had memorized the rug's pattern.

She peeked around her.

Bookcases covered any wall space that wasn't devoted to the hearth, to windows, or to the large map behind his lordship's desk. She read York and Sheffield and guessed that it depicted the north of England. The wealth of books in this isolated corner of the moorland surprised Elizabeth. The bindings looked weathered by time and many hands.

A long table occupied the floor beneath the window wall. The rainy panes gave a blurred view of the desolate moor rising behind the house. Behind her was the cheerily dancing fire that fought the room's chill. The desk before her was cluttered with three open ledgers and spills of spindled paper, a neat stack of foolscap to the left of the blotter. In the baron's chair, a grey cat licked its paws.

The cat couldn't be bothered to examine her.

But a greymalken! For the strangest reason, that cat gave Elizabeth hope.

Little else about this opportunity gave her hope. The agency's director had doubted she would be acceptable. He'd presented her detriments: too young, too pretty, too well-dressed, too quick with her opinion. She could change only the last of those, and she refused to rid her wardrobe of perfectly suitable clothes.

Then the director had presented Feldstone Grange's detriments: too remote, too unfriendly to Londoners, too detailed with his requirements for the housekeeper position. Elizabeth didn't intend to remain long-term; once her father and brother returned from the war, she would keep their lodgings. Until then, she needed work to occupy her, and the salary at the Grange would build a tidy nest egg. She didn't inform the director of her plans.

Until the coach dropped her in Widderby and the wagon trundled over a long road to the Grange, she hadn't really understood the word *remote*. The old Greystone manor perched on a rising hill before the massive moor. Should the baron refuse her employment, they would have to offer her supper and breakfast and a place to lay her head before sending her back to Widderby. The land around the Grange looked well tilled, with pastures of cattle and sheep.

The moor brooded over everything, rocky and barren of all but heather. On this early spring day, frigid wind blew from the heights. The slaty clouds hinted at snow.

That old man had taken one look at Elizabeth without her rain-draggled bonnet and judged her incapable of the housekeeper's position. She hoped Baron Harcourt would not be so hasty.

She had inquired in London before she set out and again at Sheffield, York, and Thirsk, but little could she discover about the baron. The family had held Feldstone Grange and the region for centuries. Burnt-out ruins lay closer to Widderby. "New manor," the carter had declared once the ruins came in view.

She had studied the blackened walls, the towers at the corners, reminiscent of the Tower of London. The pub host had said the Grange would be the grey-stoned building after the ruins. After the fire, the family had returned to the old Grange, with its sturdy stones.

Long and stolid, windows scattered along its breadth of the building. Multiple chimneys smoked at one end while no smoke drifted from the others. The Grange would be a nightmare for a maid to clean. Half-flights of stairs must access twisted passages. Damp rooms had hearths that would barely dissipate the cold. The unused end of the building would still need to be checked regularly.

Once inside, the entrance hall removed many of her fears about the house. Square and dominated by a stair with one landing, its painted walls held the weapons that often decorated old houses. Banners and family portraits brightened the entrance. Vividly painted doors led to four other rooms. She had looked around with obvious enjoyment. Several sconces and candelabra cast away the day's gloom. While the flagstones looked dull and heavy, painted panels beneath the stairway led to a crossing for a back hall and more vividly painted doors. The stairs led to a well-lit open salon with corridors to either wing.

The décor would be the influence of the current baron and his father, perhaps his grandfather. Elizabeth had learned that the current Lord Harcourt had served king and country for several years, leaving the Grange to the tending of his steward. His father's death in the previous year had recalled him to England. He'd spent the following Season in London, searching for a bride, only to return without one. He had no siblings, just a cousin. Beyond that, she'd discovered nothing about her potential employer.

She could assume, however. Whatever Lord Harcourt was like, he'd obviously been desperate for a housekeeper. The agency director complained that she would be the sixth in as many months. He had no explanation for their departure. That whiskered old man had claimed she wouldn't last a week. She wished to prove him and the agency director wrong.

The grey cat jumped onto the desk then to the floor. It prowled close to Elizabeth without nearing her then curled up before the fire.

A boy came in to renew the fire with coals. He started when he spotted her then ducked his head. He didn't look at her again. He lighted a lamp at the desk then scurried out.

Gawking, the older man had said. She must remember to avoid that.

Full dark came. The rising moor looked a blacker bulk against the starry night.

Then the door opened once again.

Elizabeth straightened her spine. Mindful of a good impression, she stared at the rug.

"Hicks," the man shouted into the hall. He waited, then footsteps approached. "Has she been standing here this whole while? I daresay she was soaked through when she arrived."

"Aye, your lordship, she were." The voice belonged to the whiskered man.

"Did you think to give her hot tea? Fetch a pot. Bring something sustaining."

"Aye, your lordship."

Mr. Hicks left, his steps quickly muffled. The baron passed her with quick strides, speaking as he neared. "My apologies. They did not inform me that you had arrived until I came in from the fields." He sat in his seat.

"I have not waited that long, Lord Harcourt. An hour and a little more, that is all."

"Nevertheless——." He didn't complete that. In the upper edge of her vision, she saw the ledgers shifted. Papers rustled. "Miss Elizabeth Fortescue. You are applying for the housekeeper position?"

"Yes, my lord."

"You do not look old enough to have worked in five different households in five years. You must have started very young."

Her gaze lifted before she could control it. She saw a long narrow face, a flash of dark eyes, and a faded scar slashing down his cheek, a sword cut, obviously gained in battle. Long dark hair, the ends still wet, flowed over his wide shoulders. His white linen shirt looked stark against his tanned skin. Handsome, except for the scar. From her days following the drum, she knew the nature of sword wounds: garish red and inflamed for several months, even after the fever left.

Lord Harcourt didn't catch her look, for he was staring at the papers that the agency had sent, the one with her qualifications, the second with her recommendations. Elizabeth quickly returned her gaze to the rug and answered his comment about her age. "I entered service as a housekeeper at fifteen, my lord."

"Fifteen!"

"My father's man-of-business gave me shelter when I returned from Portugal. His household was woefully mismanaged. When the housekeeper left, I assumed the management of it, and he proceeded to pay me."

"That is Mr. Severest? His recommendation is glowing. I assume the housekeeper didn't like your attempts to correct her mismanagement. Why did you leave his employment?"

"His wife returned from Ireland. She'd spent several months there, assisting her elderly parents."

"You stayed with Mr. and Mrs. Francis Beauchamp for ten months."

"Until her confinement ended and she was able to resume management of their household."

"The Tremaines give an adequate recommendation, certainly not glowing." He glanced up, catching her peeking. She saw his mouth twist before she dropped her gaze.

"Lady Tremaine dismissed me after a few months. My interactions with her family were … difficult, shall we say?"

"A son?" he hazarded.

"No, my lord. Their children were too young to have any interactions with me."

"Tremaine himself? Sir *Henry* Tremaine?"

She didn't respond. Sir Henry Tremaine's attentions were not worthy of mentioning—although she did not encounter difficulties from Lady Tremaine until she asked that she not take orders from him. Lord Harcourt did not need to know that.

When he realized she wasn't going to answer, he asked, "Lady Millingrove? I see the agency listed you were there over a year and a line is here from a Chesterton, yet her ladyship does not provide a recommendation."

"She is deceased, my lord. Last quarter. At her solicitor's request I remained in employment there until the house was purchased."

"You did not wish to work for the man that purchased the house?"

"No, Lord Harcourt."

He settled back into his chair, his gaze assessing. She could clearly envision what he saw. A woman of 20, rain-bedraggled, her red hair still darkened by the water, her skin pale and lightly freckled. Her youth he'd complained of. What else would he find to reject her application? Not her qualifications, certainly.

"Where is your family?"

"My father and my brother are both in Portugal. My father is a field officer."

"Major Fortescue? I believe I have heard of him."

"He recently received a promotion to major, my lord. My brother is a lieutenant on Colonel Wellesley's staff."

"Where is your mother, Miss Fortescue?"

"No longer with us, my lord."

"The occasion of your return from Portugal?"

She nodded without answering. He returned to studying the agency's letter. "Lord Harcourt," she thought it wise to say, "I am more than qualified for this position. I managed our household in Portugal after my mother fell ill. You see my recommendations here in England. Please do not prejudge me based upon my youth. I will say frankly that I need this opportunity, and apparently you need a housekeeper."

His mutter sounded like something her brother Alexander would say.

The door opened, admitting a maid with a tea tray. "Here," he said, "on the desk," and he dropped the ledgers to the floor. She winced at the loud thuds.

The maid slid the tray onto his desk. A ceramic teapot with steam coming from the spout, two cups, two small plates, and a larger plate with an array of sandwiches. Her mouth watered. A fresh chill shivered her. The maid went out. She'd kept her eyes on the tray the entire time. Not once had she looked at her master.

"You be mother." Lord Harcourt sounded more like an old friend than an employer. "Use that chair," he pointed to the wingback before the desk. When both sat with teacups, the heat wafting into the air and the aroma tantalizing with its promise, he cleared his throat.

Her gaze came up and encountered his dark eyes. He didn't berate her, and Elizabeth wondered if the order for a lowered gaze came from him.

"We've had trouble with our past few housekeepers."

"The agency informed me. I would be the sixth in as many months." She sipped the hot brew and felt the welcome heat begin to warm her. "What occasioned their leaving?"

He looked down at his tea then sipped before setting cup and saucer on the blotter. "The last three gave no reasons. The first two—I must say that I had problems with them. Problems not related to their position." His color heightened.

Perhaps attractive young men of rank and wealth had problems similar to young and attractive housekeepers. She decided to sidestep that issue. "I am well acquainted with managing various types of household, Lord Harcourt. Granted, my paid positions were in London. In Portugal, we had a quartermaster from whom we could requisition supplies. Here, I would need to coordinate with your factotum to request supplies."

"That would be Hicks, whom you've met. Factotum, butler, whatever I've needed. He survived my father and grandfather as well. I assume, in London, that the staffs you managed were not large."

She tallied the servants for him: the footmen and maids, upstairs and down, the cook and her helpers, the errand boy, the occasional handyman. She didn't coachmen or gardeners, rightly guessing those additions wouldn't impress him, even though she'd often given them orders from her employers.

The numbers of servants that he listed surprised her. The household servants were scant while the kitchen staff had one maid too many. She had no idea of the gardening or stable staffs or the fields, but those would not be her purview. When she pointed out the lack of house servants, he frowned, his first true one. "I do not entertain, Miss Fortescue. Managing the house staff, running the Grange, these are your sole duties."

"My lord, my chief concern will be your continued comfort."

That answer received no response from him. He picked up a ledger from the floor and found a page near the back. Leaving the ledger open to that page, he transferred it to the fore of the desk. A sheet of foolscap followed, then the quill and a silver embossed inkwell. "There remains, Miss Fortescue, only proof that you can keep accounts." The ledger page was for four months ago. He pointed to the left side. "Tot up this column," he challenged.

Elizabeth hoped her inhalation was not as sharp as it sounded in her ears. Her ciphering was impressive; she'd always bested her brother Alexander. She seemed on the verge of winning the position.

As she leaned over the desk, she caught the scent of clean sweat mixed with bay, of leather and horse. That was no reason for her heart to race.

The numbers varied. Most were simple addition; a few needed multiplying. At the bottom of the column, to the right, was a greater number. The household tally, she guessed. The items included household goods, bought in quantity. Kitchen items: salt, flour, spices, wine, three kegs of ale, another of—. She stopped her survey and touched the un-inked quill to the item. "Six kegs of beer, but the total is multiplied for eight." Her gaze lifted and looked directly at him, also leaning forward. "Do you wish me to correct or factor the incorrect total?"

The lantern cast an amber glow over the strong bones of his face. He'd missed a spot while shaving. "The number as intended," he rumbled, which was no reason for her toes to tighten in her damp shoes.

Totting up numbers did not pose any difficulties. She wondered at the former housekeepers. Had they been unnumbered? The lord's factotum, Mr. Hicks, was he illiterate, and that portion of his position fell to the housekeeper? Someone had obviously intended to steal from Baron Harcourt.

She glanced up once and found him watching, sharp as a hunting hawk.

Elizabeth wrote her figures in her decided hand, two tallies and a third that listed the difference in amount. She stared at the numbers for scant seconds then handed the sheet across the desk. Since she'd already broken Mr. Hicks' injunction not to look at the lord, she kept her eyes on him.

He drew a sheet from underneath the stacked foolscap, additional figuring which he compared to hers. Then he gave a brief nod and set aside the sheets. "You're quick and accurate."

She returned the quill to the inkstand. The nub needed sharpening. She'd tend to that if he hired her. "The agency did not mentioned counting work as part of my duties, Lord Harcourt."

"You will do what I tell you to do, when I tell you to do it."

Is that growl an attempt to frighten me? Starvation was far more frightening. Yet those words did take a step further to hiring her. "Yes, my lord."

"Hicks will give you my instructions. You will convey any matters needing my attention through him."

Ah, the sticking point. "No, my lord," she said quietly but firmly.

"No?"

"No." She met his dark eyes directly. "At the Tremaines, the butler had an animus to me. He refused to present my concerns and questions to Lady Tremaine. He gave them to Lord Tremaine, and issues were not addressed in a timely manner. I asked repeatedly to report to Lady Tremaine. She was rather languid, but I merely needed a *yes* or *no* to my proposed solutions." She realized she twisted her hands and drew them apart, curling her fingers over her knees. "The whole household, from family and through the staff, was most contentious."

Lord Harcourt winced. He pushed back from the desk and stood up. Giving her his back, he stared at the large map behind his desk. "Doubtless Harry Tremaine created opportunities to meet with his pretty, young housekeeper. He was a rattling loose screw when I knew him. I daresay he hasn't changed his ways. You are well out of that household."

"Yes, my lord. I much preferred my time with Lady Millingrove."

"You've no desire to return to Portugal?"

"I would love to return to my family. My father refuses to allow it. He says that Lord Wellesley will only increase his attacks against the French army. Until Napoleon is defeated, I must do more for my upkeep than subsist on the funds dispersed from my father's man-of-business. My father has not lived in England for many years, my lord. He does not understand the cost of things."

"Few do." He turned. "You are unsuitable in many respects, Miss Fortescue."

"Trust me, my lord. Granted I am young, but I will manage your household to keep you in comfort. I meet your qualifications, including the ability to maintain accurate ledgers. And I do not have designs upon your person."

He laughed, a short bark, then shook his head. "The gossips will say that I have designs upon *you*, Miss Fortescue."

Elizabeth laughed. "Then we shall prove them wrong, Lord Harcourt."

He sank into his chair. "Continue to laugh at the gossip, Miss Fortescue, and we will survive the first month. Ring the bell."

She found it beside the hearth, as expected, then came back to her former position on the rug. "Am I hired then, my lord?"

"You are. Woe betide those who question it."

Mr. Hicks scowled when informed that Elizabeth would be the new housekeeper. He goggled when Lord Harcourt added, "You and she will see to the supplies. Miss Fortescue will keep the ledgers. And she will report any of her concerns directly to me."

"My lord, that's not how it's been done."

"A minor change, Hicks. Cook can also convey his problems to her. That will relieve you of that burden."

The man didn't quite know what expression to put on. He settled for muttering, "Obliged, my lord."

Those dark eyes returned to Elizabeth. "Shall we say Monday and Friday mornings for our conferences? You will bring the household ledgers at those times."

She curtsied and stepped back, feeling herself dismissed.

But Lord Harcourt had one final word. "Keep your humor, Miss Fortescue. You will need it."

Find *The Dark Lord* **here**:

https://books2read.com/u/38yprZ

Trailer to come with the duology *Perils in Lace and Hard Iron*.

Opening to "Memory of Magic"

From M.A.Lee's pen name for historical fantasy, Edie Roones, the opening of a short story in the **Wild Sherwood** series, "Memory of Magic", from the collection *Out of Wild Sherwood*.

The Faerie hunter Fenric stumbles upon slaughtered deer, killed for neither food nor sport. The trail leads the Faerie beyond Sherwood and to a freehold stinking of evil.

Fenric stopped when he ran into the quiet. Breathing hard, he sought the strangeness. A few steps back, he'd heard birds, distant chirps and songs and calls. Here, all was silent.

Fae sense gave him the living heartbeats all around, a few close and beating rapidly. He peered at the trees and saw little birds tucked close to the trunks, hiding from a predatory owl or a raptor.

Then he smelled blood and ran toward it rather than away, as only

Faerie sentinels roaming Sherwood did. The coppery stench overwhelmed all other odors.

Ahead, sunlight blazed into a clearing. There, the trouble was there. Fenric slowed.

He skirted the clearing, looking for movement. An odd enchantment hovered, shimmering the light. With an intent stare he scoped the clearing, but he couldn't see anything but the grasses. Assured of no one lurking, he eased through the verge, slipping between vines tangled over two dead bushes. The enchantment resisted him, but it broke under his pressure. The shimmering light faded. The spell wasn't strong. That eased his caution—until he saw the dead deer.

Two does, pale of hide. Beyond them, a fawn. Brought down by arrows, then their throats slit. Blood soaked the ground. He studied the arrows' fletching, but he didn't recognize it. This foul deed, then, was not the work of Robin's outlaws or the sheriff's rangers that roamed Sherwood.

He seized an arrow and drew it out.

Magic erupted from the arrowhead as soon as it cleared skin. The sickly green energy flickered then vanished, gone between one breath and the next, flitting away to dissipate in little sparks of evil.

Fenric shuddered. He had to be careful with the next arrow. Hoping to trap that foul energy, he set a sphere of magic where the arrow penetrated the skin. The arrowhead eased into the sphere. It still exploded when it left the deer, but his sphere caught the foul spell before it escaped into the air.

Breaking off the iron arrowhead below his sphere, he dropped the arrow with the other one, discarded on the ground. He peered closely at the spell. It dissipated as he studied it, as quickly as the other had, but he caught the spell's purpose, to fly straight to the deer, to sink deep into a vital organ, not to kill but to incapacitate.

The spellweaver had wanted to use a knife for the actual death.

He gathered up both arrows then went to the fawn, the sphere bobbing along. The little deer was so young, too young to flee when its mother fell. No arrow had brought it down. The weaver had seized it then killed it. A quick death.

He hated the spellweaver.

He blasted the arrows apart. Only the iron arrowhead escaped his magic. He set a slower spell over the three dead deer, to hasten their decay. They would bypass rot. Their flesh and organs would crumble into ash before any predators feasted upon them. Only their hides would remain, flattened over the bones, hidden by the quick-growing grasses.

Then a stag bugled.

Fenric straightened.

At the edge of the clearing, between the two bushes that Fenric had threaded through, stood a white hart. A majestic rack crowned his head, attesting to the hart's health and power.

Blood crossed the stag's chest, but no wound marred its hide.

Then Fenric saw blood on the highest antler tips. The stag had charged the spellweaver and inflicted wounds. Had he trampled the enchanter?

The stag picked his way into the clearing, giving Fenric a chance to see the hooves were unblooded.

The white hart reached the first doe, her hide already sunken as Fenric's spell worked its magic. The stag nosed the doe's body. He snorted. Then he stepped gingerly to the fawn, little more than hide and bones as it decayed more rapidly than its mother. The stag turned to Fenric and bugled again.

Not enough blood stained the antler tips to have penetrated deeply. To gain that bloody stain across his chest, the stag must have barreled into the spellweaver.

He saluted the stag. "Hail, O great king of the forest. You fought a brave battle against an enchanter."

The stag didn't move. He stared down his snout at Fenric.

"I would find this enchanter. We two can have revenge for this foul deed."

The stag lowered his head with that large rack of antlers. Fenric didn't move as the antlers closed around him. The veriest touch to his shoulders, then the stag backed away. In a blinding flash of white, the stag sprang from the clearing.

Fenric ran after the white hart.

The deer ran for a mile, for longer, then stopped abruptly. Fenric pounded up, hard-pressed to match the hart's pace.

On the trail beyond the hart was blood.

He saw burnt leaves and scorched bark. The enchanter had fought back. Again he scanned the hart but still saw no wounds.

The fire would have caused the stag to retreat. Even magical animals feared flames.

But the hart had gifted to him the enchanter's blood. He touched a stain on his tunic.

A flicker of that foul magic woke. It gave a trace of direction. North, northwest. A labored heartbeat, heavy breaths, a halting gait. The enchanter would have used the lifeforce stolen from the deer to protect himself and to heal himself. His venture into Sherwood to steal power had turned futile. He would flee Sherwood now, returning to his lair until his healing was complete.

He must be dealt with before then.

Fenric didn't fear the enchanter. Fae magic was more powerful than any spell a pathetic human would weave. He'd heard tales of the great enchanter Merlin, the most powerful human that Faeries knew. Even Merlin's spells were nothing against Faeries.

Yet the enchanter might have other tricks to use. Iron, silver and salt, an extract of poppy, mirrors to confuse. Should his hunt take him into a human town, Fenric would need a glamour to hide himself from other humans, splitting the power he wielded against the enchanter.

But none of that would stop Fenric.

"I will track him, O king of deer. I will bring him back for your punishment or kill him where he lairs. You will have vengeance."

Find *Memory of Magic* **here**: https://books2read.com/u/47PKva

Watch the trailer for *Out of Wild Sherwood* here: https://youtu.be/ENKYL_Qi9u4

www.ingramcontent.com/pod-product-compliance
Lightning Source LLC
Chambersburg PA
CBHW051924240626
47153CB00004B/1356